What MAGiC is this?

What MAGIC is this?

HOLLY BOURNE

Barrington Stoke

First published in 2019 in Great Britain by
Barrington Stoke Ltd
18 Walker Street, Edinburgh, EH3 7LP

www.barringtonstoke.co.uk

Text © 2019 Holly Bourne

A CIP catalogue record for this book is available
from the British Library upon request

ISBN: 978-1-78112-885-5

Printed in China by Leo

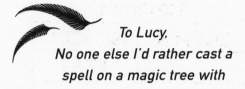

To Lucy,
No one else I'd rather cast a
spell on a magic tree with

CHAPTER ONE

So telekinesis is totally harder than I thought it would be.

I stare at my eyeliner pencil on the carpet, squinting, using all my concentration to make it move.

Move, eyeliner pencil. Go on. Roll onto your side. You can do it. I believe in you.

My brain hurts and it feels like it's about to pop a vein. But I keep going. I can sense a twitch coming. Surely the pencil must be about to move? I've been staring at it for ten minutes.

Come on. Just twitch. MOVE, YOU STUPID

EYELINER PENCIL. CAN'T YOU FEEL MY BULGING BRAIN VEIN WANTING IT SO?

Yet the pencil stays still, determined not to move. I can't believe it. I mean, I know it sounds a bit up myself, but I've always assumed, ever since reading *Matilda*, that I totally have the power to move objects with my mind. And that the only reason I haven't done it yet is because I've never given telekinesis the proper time and attention.

But here I am, on the night of a Super Blood Wolf Moon, dressed up like a sexy Wiccan. I'm ready to finally embrace my natural witchness, but ... my inner witch is not obeying. This is quite annoying and actually doesn't bode well for everything I have planned for this evening.

The doorbell rings, echoing around the house. I hear Mum call, "I'll get it!" and I let her. One more try ...

I stare at the eyeliner again.

Move ... just move ... come on, you big fat eyeliner pencil. Just roll a bit ...

I hear voices and greetings and the thud of someone running up the stairs, but I stay focused. Squinting ... wishing ...

My bedroom door flies open just as the eyeliner rolls over slightly.

OH MY GOD! I DID IT! I DID IT!

I snatch it up triumphantly and turn to Mia, who's standing in the doorway, looking like a Goth queen. There isn't much of her face that's not covered in eyeliner.

"I just made this pencil move," I tell her. "With my brain! I have telekinesis!" I wave the eyeliner over my head.

"Seriously?" Mia says, and raises an eyebrow, grinning.

"I think so! I've been practising all day and

it just suddenly rolled right then ..." I pause and suck on the end of the pencil. "Or it might have been the gust of wind from the door opening that moved it ..."

"Let's be honest, Sophia," Mia says. "It was most definitely that."

Mia strides in and dumps all her sleepover gear onto my bed. Her bag makes a rather worrying clanking sound as it lands on my purple duvet, like she's got multiple kitchen sinks in there.

"Hey, it may very well be the case that I'm an actual witch!" I tell her.

"Well, we'll know after tonight, won't we?" Mia replies.

She starts emptying her bag of its contents – getting out loads of candles, a ball of wool and a bunch of red roses. I get up from the carpet to look at her spoils and I pick up one of the roses.

4

"Thanks for getting me the rose I needed," I say. "Were they expensive?"

Mia points and winks at me. "They were down to only three quid in Tesco. I think they're about to die."

"Won't an almost dead rose tarnish the magic?" I ask.

"They're not dead yet. We only need them for tonight."

I hear Mum's footsteps on the stairs. "Sophia?" Mum's voice warbles. Mia and I look at each other in fear, and then to the bed, and then back to each other again.

"Quick," I whisper. "Hide the weird stuff."

Mia tugs my childhood blankie off the bed and drapes it over her witchcraft collection just as Mum pushes into my room.

"Mum, you didn't knock!" I complain.

She ignores my protest. "What the hell

have both of you done to your faces?" Mum asks, taking in our insane amount of make-up.

Mia and I both start snorting with laughter. "We're just experimenting," I say. "Trying out new looks."

Mum clips an earring onto her ear, still frowning. "I thought the point of a new look was to make you look better?" she says. "Not worse. You look like you've punched yourself in both eyes."

Cheers, Mum, I think. I twist my head to check myself in my mirror. I spent ages on this smoky-eye look. I even watched a YouTube tutorial to make sure I got it right. And my wrist hurts from all the blending I had to do.

"I think we look cool," Mia says, beaming back at her. Mum's eyes shift to Mia's long sleeves bunched over her hands. Mum bites her lip and clips on her other earring. I wonder if she's noticed Mia's new obsession with never showing her arms, but Mum doesn't comment.

"Yes, well ..." Mum says. "Anyway, Sophia, there are some pizzas in the freezer for you guys. And I got some dips and crisps like you asked for."

"Thank you," I say.

"Don't be too noisy, otherwise Ken next door will get upset."

"We won't."

"That means the TV can't go over twenty-five."

"I know."

"And call me if anything happens ..." Mum's eyes flick to Mia's covered arms again. "Anything at all."

"Mum, we're just watching movies and then sleeping," I reassure her, while thinking, *And dabbling with witchcraft using spells we found on Google.* "We won't be noisy."

7

"Hmm. OK. Well, still. Call. Any doubt, just call. I'll be back by ten tomorrow."

Mum leans in for a kiss, suffocating me with her perfume. I hope it wears off by the time she gets to the date that she's hiding from me. "Just having dinner at Sandra's," she told me. Yeah right. Not that I blame Mum for wanting to find someone new. It's been almost a year now. But, God, what does it mean if your tragic mother's love life is going better than yours? She's old and mental, while I'm in the prime of my youth. And I'm the one having to turn to magic to get a boyfriend.

I peck the air next to Mum's neck and wave her out of my room. We hear her collect her overnight bag, call goodbye up the stairs and then the click of the front door.

"Your mum out on another secret date?" Mia asks.

"She thinks I'm so stupid."

"How do you feel about it?"

I shrug. I don't really want to talk about it. "I feel like we can get the ingredients back out now," I say, lifting blankie off them.

Mia decides not to push it and screws up her face instead. "Did you just call them 'ingredients'?"

"Yeah. What else are we supposed to call them?"

"I don't know," Mia says. "But not *ingredients*. We're making spells, not a fish pie. You need to take it seriously."

I raise both eyebrows. "I am."

"Good. Otherwise the magic won't work."

I reach over and gently poke her. "Mia, I'm taking it seriously, I pro—" I break off as the doorbell goes. "That will be Alexis. I'll go let her in." I scramble off the bed and pad downstairs.

When I'm halfway down, Mia calls out, "I hope you're not going to waste our evening of magic on trying to win back Aidan."

I hold my hand to my heart at the mention of his name. *Aidan, Aidan, Aidan.* I'm addicted to hearing it. I close my eyes and feel the humiliation and pain and rejection bombard in.

"You'll have to wait and see," I call back, brushing aside my feelings.

The doorbell trills again.

"Let me in," Alexis yells into the letterbox. "I'm so cold I'm scared Hell has actually frozen over and now loads of weird stuff is going to happen out here. It's not safe."

I force a smile onto my face and let in the last member of our coven.

CHAPTER TWO

Our agreed dress code for the evening is "Outfits That Would Scare Children" and Alexis has certainly followed the brief. I open the door to see her covered in black and lace ... and more black and more lace. But her face is make-up free, her nose red and snotty.

"Hi," Alexis sniffs. She steps into the warmth of my house with her sleeping bag wedged under her armpit. "Sorry I'm a bit late. I was just leaving and then I saw Casper's water bowl, by the door, ready to go out with the bins tomorrow and ... and ..." Alexis judders into tears and leans on the wall to steady herself. I close the door and go to hug her, and she flings herself into my arms.

"Sorry," Alexis keeps saying as she makes my neck all damp. "Sorry. It's just ... it had Casper's name on it, you know? He loved that bowl."

I nod into her hair, pat her back and keep repeating, "There, there." Alexis has been sobbing on and off since her dog, Casper, died last week. This is very sad, yes. However, Mia and I have been slightly thrown, as Alexis always *hated* that dog. Like, literally hated him. Her nickname for the Yorkshire Terrier was "Crap Bag" and she complained about him all the time. His crimes against Alexis included: barking, smelling, being around her at any given moment and taking attention away from her – not that she'd ever admit that last one.

I give Alexis a final squeeze and break off the hug. "I have dips," I tell her. "So many dips."

At the sound of the word "dip", Mia appears at the top of the stairs. "Oh my God, I forgot about the dips!" she calls down. "Can we open them now?" She gallops towards us but stops when she sees the state of Alexis. "Oh, hon, what's wrong?"

Alexis shakes her head. "It's nothing. Sorry, I don't mean to be dramatic … I just … as I was leaving, I saw Casper's bowl …" She starts crying again.

I let Mia take over while I get on with arranging snacks. I pad into the kitchen and yank everything out of the fridge. Then I tip a pile of crisps into a bowl and place the dips and crisps on a tray. I hear Mia calm Alexis down and the two of them thudding back upstairs.

"I really don't mean to be dramatic," Alexis repeats as they head up. I grin to myself, as Alexis is a very dramatic person. Both my friends are. It's impossible for me not to become "the quiet one" when I hang out with these two – even a foghorn would struggle to get attention. Mia's shyer in company but pretty demanding when it's just the three of us.

I follow them up to my room, where I find Alexis much calmer, sitting down in front of my mirror so Mia can do her make-up.

"I did try to do the whole eyeliner thing," Alexis explains as I bash in with my tray and set it on the floor. "But I kept crying it off, you know? From the grief?"

Mia is leaning forward over her as she smudges my kohl pencil over Alexis's face.

"Has Sophia told you about her telekinesis moment with the eyeliner yet?" Mia asks Alexis, using her pinky finger to smudge the make-up.

"What's telekinesis?" Alexis asks, then yelps, "Ouch, Mia! You got some in my eye." Alexis bats Mia away for a moment and blinks madly.

"Telekinesis is the ability to move stuff using just your brain," I say.

"And you did what? Made your eyeliner float or something?" Alexis asks.

"Well, not exactly, but it rolled over," I tell her.

"Using the wind from the door swinging open," Mia adds, and I stick my tongue out at her.

Alexis looks unimpressed. She leans into the mirror and inspects her face. "Oh God, I look like Mia!" Alexis twists back and sees my snack assortment. "Is that Moroccan hummus? Oh my God, you STAR."

We all sit in a circle and demolish the food, spraying crumbs and dropping dollops of dip onto my carpet as we talk and eat.

I'm feeling a bit apprehensive about everything we're planning to do. The whole witch thing started as a joke, sort of. There's this show about them on Netflix we all watched together a few weeks ago. And, because it was a Sunday night and we were bored, we jokingly cast a "Sunday Snow Spell" in Mia's kitchen to cheer us up. It involved melting chocolate with marshmallows and chanting a bit and then eating the marshmallows. We'd totally made it up and it was completely stupid – until it actually snowed that night while we slept.

"We're witches," Mia messaged us the next morning, with a screen grab of the announcement that school was closed. "We did it."

"It *was* forecast to snow," I pointed out.

"Not this much."

"Yeah, but still."

Anyway, since then, Mia's got proper into witchcraft. She's been googling all these spells, wearing even more black than normal and keeps touching tree branches and leaves and stuff whenever she walks past them. I guess Mia's always had a tendency to veer towards the dark side. She's dyed her hair black since Year Seven. Her long sleeves are black and I worry that they could be covering a multitude of darknesses. She changes in a toilet cubicle after PE rather than with everyone else and she wore the long sleeves even in the summer, no matter how hot it was.

Soon all that remains of the dips is a bowl of crumbs and two empty tubs, scraped clean. We sit back on my carpet, cradling our bellies and sighing about what we've done to ourselves.

"Will the magic work if I'm this … full?" Alexis asks. She looks down at her bulging belly, strokes it and says, "Mummy is so proud." It's hilarious when Alexis stuffs herself. She looks about six months pregnant for a good few hours afterwards. Alexis looks back up at me. "Didn't you say you had pizza too?"

"HOW are you still hungry?" I screech in disbelief.

"It's the grief!" Alexis replies.

Mia claps to get our attention. "Let's get going already. We've got three spells to cast tonight and we've not even set up the magic circle yet."

Alexis is still rubbing her belly. "Can the pizza be the magic circle?"

"Honestly, how are you *still* hungry?" Mia asks.

"I told you, it's the grief!"

I stand up to stop this turning into yet another argument. I'm always caught in the middle of Mia being upset that Alexis *doesn't take her seriously*, while Alexis is upset that Mia *is too serious all the time.*

"How about I put the oven on?" I say slowly,

like they're children. "And, while I'm doing that, you two can get all the ingredients ready?"

"Ingredients?" Mia yelps at me, ruining my attempt at peacekeeping. "Ingredients? For God's sake, Sophia. None of you are taking this seriously." She throws her hands up and storms out of my bedroom.

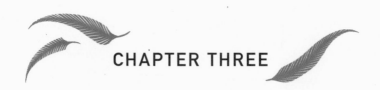

CHAPTER THREE

I look at Alexis.

Alexis looks at me.

We hear the slam and lock of the bathroom door.

"What did I do?" I ask.

Alexis rolls over onto my bed, stretching her feet out. "It's just Mia," she says. "You never have to do anything for her to react like this."

"What should we do?" I say.

"Exactly what she wants you to do. Follow her ..." Alexis replies as she shakes her head and laughs. "And Mia calls *me* the drama queen."

I stand up, unsure and annoyed. I love my

friends, I do. But between the two of them
their issues and demands, there's rarely room
left for me. Tonight was supposed to cheer me
up. *Me*. After Aidan. But now it's turned into
a frigging dead-dog vigil, mixed with dramas I
don't even understand. "Why don't you sort the
pizzas out," I suggest, "and I'll go talk to Mia?"

"A million times yes," Alexis says.

I edge out into the hallway, not sure why I'm
creeping. I hear Mia crying on the other side of
the bathroom door and my stomach squeezes.

I knock gently and her crying stutters. "Mia,
it's me," I say needlessly.

"I just want to be alone right now," Mia sniffs.

"We didn't mean to upset you."

"I'M NOT UPSET."

"Maybe you are just a tiny bit."

"NO, I'M NOT."

"You've just locked yourself in the bathroom."

"NO, I HAVEN'T."

Then I hear her laugh at herself and my stomach relaxes, knowing Mia's on her way back to normality. I do not like the thought of her being locked in a room where my razors are.

I laugh too. I wait. I listen as Mia's crying calms down, mixed with the sounds of Alexis opening and closing the oven door with gusto. I wait a bit more, letting silence work its magic. And then, with a scrape of the lock, the door swings open, revealing Mia huddled on the bathmat.

"Sorry," she says sheepishly. Her eye make-up is all over her face.

"I'm sorry too."

Mia wraps her arms around her chest. "I just ... well ... it's like you're not taking the witchcraft seriously."

"We are! I tried to move an eyeliner using only the power of my brain."

"Yeah, to take the piss," Mia says.

"No." It's the complete truth. "I really did think I was almost there. And Alexis is just hungry." I reach out an arm. "Come on. It was my idea to do this whole witch sleepover. Why would I do it if I was taking the piss?"

Mia snuffles. "It takes the piss that you only want to do it to get Dickwad Aidan back."

I bunch my hands into my eyes. "Don't call him that, please."

"It's true."

I close my eyes as the sadness hits me again, like someone has just snapped an elastic band against my heart. Aidan doesn't want me. No one ever wants me. Because I'm too nothing.

"Can we just go eat pizza and then cast some spells already?" I ask, desperate to get off the subject of Aidan.

"Promise you'll take it seriously?" Mia says.

I nod and she finally lets me hug her. I shuffle onto the bathmat and clutch Mia's scrawny frame. I can feel her heartbeat thudding through her lacy top and it's like hugging a terrified bird.

"What's going on?" I ask. "Is everything OK?"

Mia sighs and I know she won't tell me. She never does. "Yes, I'm fine."

"Sure you're sure?"

"Sophia, please."

"OK, OK, but I'm always here."

"I know, and me too. Sorry to call him a dickwad. It just makes me annoyed that he's upset you so much when you are clearly amazing."

It's weird how compliments can make you feel sad, particularly the ones you disagree with.

"Well, I'm clearly not. Otherwise he wouldn't have—"

"CAN YOU EAT PIZZA RAW?" Alexis calls up the stairs. "I'M SO HUNGRY I CANNOT WAIT ANOTHER MINUTE."

Mia and I smile, then we both stand up and walk into the hallway. "HOW ARE YOU STILL HUNGRY?" we shout down the stairs together.

"I TOLD YOU, IT'S THE GRIEF."

CHAPTER FOUR

I don't think I believed in magic until I fell in love with Aidan Chambers. Well, to be more accurate, until Aidan fell back in love with me. Everyone in school loves Aidan. It's a given. A default setting for every girl in Year Nine. One of the most controversial things you can say is, "No, I don't really fancy Aidan Chambers." And no one would believe you anyway.

People like Aidan do not fall in love with people like me. That's not how school works. That's not how life works. At least, that's not how I thought it worked.

I was resigned to loving him from afar, just like everyone else. It had its high moments – like how he'd pass me in the corridor every Tuesday between eleven-fifteen and eleven-eighteen, while I was on my way to English and he was on his way to Maths. I'd dress up every Tuesday for this occasion – doing my hair in a special style, maybe smearing on some lip tint but nothing too strong that'd get me detention. I'd practise walking attractively in my bedroom the night before, choosing what face to pull. One that looked like I was confident and pretty and fun and approachable and lovable, but not trying too hard. Then there were the low moments – where I'd walk past him every Tuesday between eleven-fifteen and eleven-eighteen, with red lips and a French plait and a really well-prepared smile attached to my face … and Aidan would just walk on past me.

This did not deter my love.

In time, Aidan will notice me, I'd tell myself at eleven-nineteen every Tuesday. *In time. When it's right.*

Until that time came, my favourite thing to do was sit and stare into nothingness, imagining how amazing it would feel to be his girlfriend, particularly during the week when he was the lead in the school play. I'd sit in the school hall, in a "reserved" chair in the front row, and after he'd bowed he'd kiss me in front of everybody ... But the months kept passing and still Aidan didn't once notice me.

That was until I did something a bit weird.

Look, so maybe this will sound mental. OK, it will definitely sound mental. But I didn't realise what was going to happen and I was in an odd mood that day. I'd only just got my period, finally. My womb was acting all like, *This is everything you've been missing out on ALL AT ONCE*, especially as I was the last girl in my form to start. I was using a giant nappy-like sanitary towel every two hours and it felt like my womb was trying to dig its way out of my body using a spoon. So, yeah, maybe it was the blood loss, or just that Chemistry was really boring, but I ... I ...

I cast a love spell on Aidan Chambers using a Bunsen burner, OK?

I was feeling crushed because it was a Tuesday and he'd ignored me again. To be fair, I hadn't made my normal effort, as I'd spent the whole of that morning before school in child's pose on the bathroom floor, howling like a cat and saying to Mum, "You mean it's going to be this bad every month for the next forty years of my life?" I'd missed the bus and Mum had had to drive me to school with crap sweaty hair. So of course Aidan hadn't noticed me. Together with all the hormones and the period, this had made me so upset that I went and cried in a toilet cubicle.

Then I had Chemistry and my partner, Nell, was off again with chronic fatigue syndrome. So I was doing an experiment alone in the corner, just like most lessons since she'd got sick two months before. We were supposed to be setting aluminium on fire, to see what colour it turned or something. The Bunsen burners were out and I was staring into the flame in front of me, thinking about how beautiful Aidan's chin is. It was then that I heard a voice in my head whisper to the rest of me: *Cast a little love spell.*

I didn't give it any thought, just ripped out a page of my Chemistry book and wrote Aidan's name with mine and a heart around them. I didn't know if that was an actual spell; it just felt right. Then I folded the paper up, kissed it, held it between the metal tongs and shoved it into the flame. It burst into a spectacular orange and I found myself whispering, "If we are supposed to be together, bring us together. Help him see me as I see him."

Then I got a horrifically bad period cramp and all the dramatic tension vanished. I had to ask to be excused and I limped out.

It was all a bit embarrassing and I didn't think much more of it – until two weeks later. I was sitting on my own again, staring at the periodic table and trying to care about halogen gases, when there was a knock on the classroom door. Aidan appeared. Every girl sat up in her seat instantly, me included. Even Miss Matthews looked a bit flushed at the sight of him.

"Hi," Aidan said to our teacher. "I've been moved into this set, but I forgot and accidentally went to my old class instead."

Every girl in the room giggled, batting their eyelashes and flicking their hair around like hippos batting off flies with their tails. Aidan Chambers looked particularly gorgeous that day – with a new cropped haircut and a stripy scarf.

Miss Matthews nodded. "Right, OK," she said. "Well, we're halfway into our lesson now. So just take a seat and try to keep up, and we can talk at the end about what you might need to catch up on."

My heart fell out of my mouth the moment I realised this meant Aidan was about to come and sit next to me. Me! ME? I had the only available space. Oh God. Why hadn't I washed my hair that morning? Why had I drawn weird vines all over my hands in biro during Geography earlier? Did I smell? What if I smelled? How could I check I didn't smell without him noticing? I was just shoving my hand up my jumper to swipe under my armpits to smell my hand, when Aidan appeared at my side.

"Hi," he whispered, grinning. "Can I sit here?"

I still had my hand inside my jumper. We were sharing our first words with my hand shoved in my armpit. I couldn't talk. My tongue wouldn't work. I tried to open my mouth to say something normal and simple and appropriate like "of course". But all I could manage was this small squeak and shrug.

Aidan slid in next to me and started rummaging in his backpack for his book. I snuck a look at him and, oh my, he was so beautiful.

He sat upright and looked at me.

"You OK?" Aidan asked.

I nodded again. My hand was still in my armpit.

"I'm Aidan by the way."

I know that, I KNOW THAT, I thought. I know your surname and your star sign and how compatible it is with my star sign. Very, since you're asking. I know that you have a younger sister in Year Seven. I know that you had your hair cut over half term. I know that you're left-handed.

"Oh, hi, I'm Sophia."

It was a miracle that I was able to get those words out.

"Cool. Nice to meet you," he whispered, smiling.

It had happened. It had finally happened. Aidan Chambers knew I existed. Level unlocked.

"Oh, yeah, nice to meet you too."

CHAPTER FIVE

Back at the sleepover, we are finally ready to cast some serious spells. Alexis has wolfed down most of the pizza. We've all applied appropriate amounts of eyeliner and promised not to set each other off crying any more.

"Has everyone gone to the toilet?" Mia asks. "I don't want our magic circle interrupted by one of you needing a wee."

"We can't go for a wee if we need one?" Alexis asks.

Mia shakes her head. "No."

"What madness is this?"

"It's MAGIC – we need to concentrate."

I put my hand up. "Yes, Sophia?" Mia says, like she's a teacher calling on me in class.

"Umm, well, I didn't need a wee, but now I do because you've made me think about it."

"Me too," Alexis says.

Mia throws her head back. "For God's sake, by the time you two are finally ready, the Super Blood Wolf Moon will be over already."

"So are we allowed to go for a wee?" Alexis asks.

"If you must."

I check my phone as I lean on the wall outside the bathroom, waiting for Alexis to wee first. Aidan Chambers hasn't messaged. Not since the last time I checked, which was ten minutes ago, while the other two were busy sorting through Mia's ingredients. And he hadn't messaged the time I checked five minutes before

36

that, when I was clearing up the pizza crusts from the carpet. In fact, despite my determined checking, Aidan has not messaged me in two whole weeks.

I close my eyes and make myself concentrate.

Message me, message me, message me, I command the universe. I picture Aidan at Lucy's party tonight. I know he is there, because I checked his profile at least twelve times today. I picture Aidan feeling sad at the party, like something is missing, but it takes him a while to figure out what. I picture him laughing with his friends but then staring into space, sadly, and realising he misses me. I picture him standing up and telling his friends to wait a minute, and then going out into the cold garden. I picture him writing me a message – because he has to let me know right away what a mistake he has made.

Message me, message me, message me.

The toilet flushes; the door opens. Alexis comes out holding her stomach.

"It's all yours," she says, and stands to one side so I can get past. "Why did you let me eat all that pizza?" she groans. "I'm going to be digesting it for the rest of my life."

I leave my phone on the bannister when I go to wee, but it has no messages on it. My visualisation didn't work. I need to cast this spell. It's the only chance I have left.

CHAPTER SIX

When I return to my bedroom, it's transformed into some kind of Halloween haunted house. Mia's been busy while we were peeing. There are candles everywhere, lit and flickering, and Mia's sitting in a giant circle she's made out of tealights. She's using a compass app on her phone so we can see where north, south, east and west are. She's switched off all my lights and it's black and pretty spooky and witchy.

"Are you ready?" Mia asks as I stop in shock in the doorway. She sees my phone clutched in my hand and adds, "Phone off."

"But yours is still on," I object.

"Only because we need to know where north is. It's on do not disturb."

Alexis holds both palms up and shrugs at me. "She's made me put mine in my bag."

I mime switching mine off, not wanting to start another argument. But there's no way I'm actually turning it off, not when Aidan could ring to declare his undying love at any moment.

"Thank you," Mia says. "Now, sit down and let's form the circle."

I fold my legs under myself and join them on the carpet, then absent-mindedly reach out to hold my finger in a candle flame for a second.

I hope this works.

"Right, we all need to hold hands in order to cast a circle," Mia instructs us.

"Why do we need to cast a circle?" Alexis asks.

"It makes the magic stronger."

"Okey dokey," I say, and hold out my palms.
I really want to giggle and I can tell Alexis does
too.

"Eww, Lexi, your hands are all sticky from
pizza," I say.

"Sorry. I washed them in the loo but then I
found a leftover slice. Hang on." She rubs them
on her lacy outfit. "That better?"

I wrinkle my nose. "Sort of."

Mia eyeballs both of us. "Are you two done
already?"

We nod and clasp our hands tighter to hold
in our laughter.

"Right, so there are four elements but only
three of us," Mia says, "so I don't mind being two
elements. Which element do you want to be?"

"Umm, what's an element again?" Alexis asks,
while Mia rolls her eyes. God, she really is in a
cranky mood tonight.

"Earth, fire, water and air."

"Oh, right, cool," Alexis says. "Can I be fire?"

I feel my stomach twist, as I kind of wanted to be fire.

"Yep, of course. Sophia? What element do you want?"

It's not a question I'm used to being asked and I struggle as I consider them in my head. I'm trying to figure out which element feels most "me", besides fire. Not earth, I don't think. I don't like getting dirty. Maybe air? I do like it when it's proper windy outside. I always go out and stand in it and have deep and meaningful thoughts.

"Air," I say.

"Right, that makes me earth and water. They're a bit conflicting, but I'm sure it won't damage the spell too much." Mia reaches into her bag and hands two items over to us. Alexis gets a match and I get a really gross feather that looks like it fell out of a dying pigeon.

"Umm, thanks for the present?" I say, deadpan.

"It's a representation of your element," Mia explains, pulling out a lump of moss and a travel bottle of Evian. "Right, I'll say some stuff and you have to repeat it after me and then put your element down in front of you to form a circle. Ready?"

"Ready," we chorus.

Mia closes her eyes, and Alexis and I look at each other to check if we need to copy her.

"Close your eyes," Mia instructs.

We do, but we both start giggling.

"Stop laughing," Mia snaps.

"Sorry," I say, still laughing.

We giggle ourselves out, but it takes a good few minutes and another telling-off from Mia.

"Why aren't you taking this seriously? Sophia, tonight was YOUR idea."

"I know, I know …" I start laughing again. "I've just got the giggles, that's all."

"You have to take it seriously. Intention is really important in magic."

The thought that I could ruin my spell calms me down. We eventually settle and hold hands again, close our eyes again. I let myself sink into the darkness. *This could work*, I tell myself. Then Aidan will be mine again and my heart won't constantly hurt any more – the anguish and pain and longing and feeling like nobody ever wants me will be gone.

Mia starts talking in this really loud, spooky voice. "Spirits of Mother Nature, I call on you," she booms out. "We ask that you keep everyone in this circle safe. Spirits of earth, I call on you." There's a big silence, then Mia says, "Sophia, you're next. Air is east on the compass."

"Oh, right," I say, with my eyes still closed.
"Umm. Spirits of air, I call on thee," I say.

"Why did you just say *thee?*" Alexis asks,
cracking up. "You sound like a witch from
Macbeth!"

"I dunno," I say. "It felt right. Anyway, I call
on YOU," I correct myself. I feel around for the
grubby dead pigeon feather and chuck it in front
of me.

"Lex, it's you," Mia says.

"OK, cool. Spirits of fire, I call on you."

"Spirits of water, I call on you," Mia finishes.
"Mother Nature, we have called upon your
elements and we ask you to guide us and help
our intentions come true. Again, please keep
everyone in this circle safe ..."

That's the moment it stops being funny. I
suddenly feel my skin burst into prickles of

goosebumps and every hair on the back of my neck stands up. Alexis freezes next to me and I sense she's feeling it too.

"And that's it," Mia says. "The circle has been formed. Now it's time to cast our spells."

And, if it's possible, my goosebumps get even bumpier.

CHAPTER SEVEN

It's crazy how goosebumpy your skin can get even under the heat of two dozen Bunsen burner flames.

"Do you mind measuring out twenty thingies of hydrogen peroxide into this beaker?" Aidan asked, a week after joining my class.

"Hahahahahahahahahahahahahahahahaha nooooo, of course not," I replied. I don't know why I was laughing hysterically, but I was.

Aidan somehow seemed to find my uncontrollable giggles endearing. "You're cute," he stated, just like that, and I'm not sure how I managed to not drop the beaker full of hydrogen peroxide onto the floor.

"Thanks. You're cute too," I said automatically.

That's when I *did* drop the beaker. It smashed everywhere, loudly, with liquid and glass splashing the ground. The class stopped, stared and laughed.

"Get back, get back!" Miss Matthews yelled. She ran over with her arms out, shooing me and Aidan away while I withered and died with humiliation. "Has it got on your skin, Sophia?" Miss Matthews asked me. "Or your clothes? It might have burned a hole in your uniform."

I backed away and checked myself. "I ... I ... I don't think so."

"How about you, Aidan?" our teacher asked.

I shot an embarrassed glance at him. He was trying to stop himself laughing, biting on his sexy fist. I couldn't believe I said he was cute too. What was wrong with me? It just kind of fell out. Oh God, I wanted to die. I wanted to die so badly that I would've drunk the hydrogen peroxide if it wasn't all over the floor.

"We need to get a lab technician here to clean this up properly." Miss Matthews pointed at us. "You two, move your chairs away and wait." She then turned and clapped to get our class into order. "And the rest of you can get on with your experiments … in SILENCE please."

I dragged my stool away meekly, my nostrils burning, Aidan following. Miss Matthews used the class phone to summon someone. I couldn't talk. I could hardly breathe. I sat down and put my head in my hands, swearing silently to myself.

But Aidan seemed utterly unbothered by the whole palaver. In fact, he seemed to be enjoying it. He leaned back, stretched out his legs and surveyed the room, which bustled with everyone getting back to work.

"So you think I'm cute then?" Aidan asked, a smirk on his perfect face.

There wasn't much of me left to still turn red, but I managed it.

"Sorry I messed up the experiment," I said, dodging his question.

"The way I see it," Aidan continued, "is there's a very simple outcome from this kind of mutual attraction. If two people think the other one is cute, they normally ... you know ..." He shrugged. "Go out on a date or something."

WHAT WAS HAPPENING?

Aidan Chambers was suggesting we go on a date. AIDAN ACTUAL CHAMBERS. This couldn't be real! Was this really my spell with the page from my Chemistry book?! Aidan didn't even know me! We'd only spoken twice in Chemistry since he joined my set, as I'd been too nervous to function – once that first day when he'd introduced himself and then when he'd asked to borrow my pencil sharpener. But somehow this had cast some kind of magic on him. He now knew that I a) existed, and b) was the sort of person who owned a pencil sharpener. And he liked that I existed and I had a pencil sharpener and he was ASKING ME ON A DATE? Hang on, wasn't he seeing Bella Morris? I thought they were back together again? I'd seen them kissing by the school gates. But surely not. I couldn't believe this was happening. Had Aidan noticed me all those times in the corridor before? Had he been too shy up until now? Had all my French plaits and attractive walking paid off? Or, oh my God, was it my love spell coming true? Was I really a witch after all? Holy cowbags, that was a *lot* of responsibility to suddenly be thinking about. I needed to make sure I used my powers for good ...

"Umm ..." Aidan Chambers said, interrupting my internal freak-out. "Normally people reply to those kinds of questions. You know, out loud?"

"Oh." I hadn't said a word. I was just sort of shaking and breathing very heavily.

The door swung open and a lab technician arrived, adorned in a white coat, gloves and goggles.

"Where's the spillage?" the technician asked.

Miss Matthews pointed over to us as I raised my hand sheepishly.

"Over here," I said. "It was me. Sorry, I'm so sorry."

The technician shrugged and snapped her gloves on. "Hey, it happens. But stay over there."

She bent down and got to work on mopping up my huge accident. The air smelled of bleach, and chemicals itched my nostrils. I scratched my nose and wondered if I was just hallucinating from the fumes.

"You've still not said anything," Aidan Chambers told me. "I'm starting to feel a bit embarrassed now."

I looked over at his perfect face and his perfect hand buried into his perfect head of hair. This was too insane. I didn't think my heart would beat regularly ever again, but I was loving it.

"I guess we could go do something," I said at last, wondering how on earth I was going to break this news to Mia and Alexis in a way that meant they would actually believe me. ("I can't believe all your stalking paid off," Mia told me later. "That shouldn't be rewarded.")

"Great." Aidan grinned, all casual. "How about after school? We could go get a milkshake?"

"*Today?*"

That soon? THAT SOON? But I didn't have a change of clothes. But I needed to mentally prepare. But life wasn't ever this dramatic. Well, at least not normally. It must be the spell, it must, it must.

"Yes, today," Aidan replied. "Why not today? You're not busy, are you?"

"No," I said. I mean, even if I'd had an appointment to meet God and he'd promised to answer all of life's most pressing questions, I still would have cancelled it to go get a milkshake with Aidan Chambers. "Not busy. A milkshake sounds great."

We put our numbers into each other's phones while Miss Matthews wasn't looking, like that was normal. And when I ran out afterwards for an emergency crisis meeting with the girls in the English-block toilets, he messaged.

Aidan Actual Chambers messaged me:

Meet you at gates after school? X

We all squealed like pigs at a squealing convention. Then Mia and Alexis helped me with my hair and make-up, and we rehearsed how to suck a milkshake sexily, and how to make conversation without me revealing that I already knew everything about him.

"You cannot reveal the extent of your obsession," Mia said. "It will terrify him."

"But Aidan said the only thing that scares him is fear itself," I said. "Remember? It was in that interview he did for the school newspaper two years ago."

"You see," Alexis said. "No one else but you remembers that. You are terrifying."

But there was no need to rehearse any conversation. The moment I met Aidan Chambers at the school gates, he pulled me into him and kissed me. With tongue. My first kiss. Right there. No build-up, no eye contact, no romantic talk about how beautiful the stars were, which was fair enough as it was only three-fifty, so the stars weren't out.

I wasn't quite sure how to kiss back. Aidan's tongue seemed very large and plungy, and he tasted a bit too strongly of spearmint gum. Plus I was certain the whole school was watching. But who else can say their first ever kiss was with the most popular, good-looking boy in school? Not many, that's who. So I enjoyed it. I felt fireworks and butterflies and the heavens opening – all that stuff you are supposed to feel.

I must have done an OK job on the kissing front because Aidan continued to put his tongue in my mouth for the rest of the afternoon, where it soon tasted of strawberry milkshake. We didn't really talk much. We didn't really do anything other than kiss. But that was enough.

For me, at least.

It clearly wasn't enough for him. I wasn't enough for him.

Well, not until I cast another spell.

CHAPTER EIGHT

"You can open your eyes now," Mia says.

I blink away my happy memories of Aidan and my dark bedroom comes into focus. Mia looks scary with all her crazy make-up on and I almost jump. We grin at one another nervously – we're not in the mood to play up any more. I still have goosebumps from forming the circle, with every inch of my skin prickling, like I can feel the spirits close.

"Who wants to cast the first spell?" Mia asks.

Alexis puts her hand up. "I'll go," she says. "I've brought my offering and everything."

"Offering?" I ask.

We agreed that we wouldn't share our spells until tonight, not that mine isn't easy to guess. But I've been so wrapped up in researching love spells that I haven't given much thought to what my friends might cast.

I hear the shrill squeak of a bone toy and I wonder how I didn't guess Alexis's.

"Jeez, that thing is loud," Mia complains as Alexis places an old, chewed, stinky dog toy into the magic circle.

"It was his favourite," Alexis says, her voice catching. "I used to get so annoyed with Casper chewing on it and now ... now ... now I'll never hear it again." She looks up to the ceiling and blinks to stop fresh tears falling. "Can we ... can we help him to cross over? Just in case he hasn't reached doggy heaven?"

Mia reaches out and squeezes Alexis's hand

in a rare show of sympathy. "Of course we can,"
Mia says. "Do you have the spell?"

Alexis nods. "I just need to say a blessing
and offer up a sacrifice. I'm using his bone toy
for that."

"Let's do it then," I say.

Alexis lets out a big sigh, then picks up a
matchbook and strikes a match. She uses it
to light a big white candle in the middle of the
other candles. Then we join hands again, just
because it feels like the right thing to do.

"Umm, hi, Mother Nature and the spirits and
stuff," Alexis says in a much less authoritative
voice than Mia's. "So ... well ... I was just hoping
you'd, like, bless my dog, Casper, and make sure
he gets into Heaven – or whatever you have as
Heaven in Wiccan land."

Alexis sniffs. "Please bless Casper, the
greatest dog ever. I may not have appreciated

him at the time ..." She hiccups and I squeeze her hand tighter. "I could have been a better owner, but he really was a cool dog and I didn't know what I had until he was gone." Alexis starts weeping and drops our hands to reach out and start squeaking the bone toy.

I think Mia senses the drop in concentration, as she calls, "Spirits, help Casper pass over," in her wise, commanding voice, and I copy her.

"Spirits, help Casper cross over."

And, through her tears, Alexis says it too. "Spirits, help Casper pass over."

We sit, waiting, for what I'm not sure. Until Alexis jumps and yells, "Oh my God, the curtain just moved!"

We all twist our heads in the direction of my window and every part of me is tingling. I feel a breeze, but the curtain is still.

"Really?" I ask.

"Yeah, it just fluttered."

"But the windows are closed," I point out, feeling even more zingy. "Maybe it's Casper saying hi?"

"Or goodbye?" Mia suggests, which is a mistake, because that sets Alexis off again.

"Don't," Alexis sobs. "Oh, I miss him SO much. Do you think the spell worked?"

"Of course it worked," I say.

Alexis wipes under her eyes. "I wasn't sure about tonight. I never believed we made it snow and I thought it would just be a laugh to cheer you up, Sophia. But, like, I *really* felt something as I was talking about Casper. All the hairs on my skin stood up on end."

My body chills, because that's exactly what I felt too. Maybe it was magic? Or maybe I just need to turn the thermostat up? How are you supposed to tell the difference?

"I just hope it's real," Alexis says, and looks at the window. "I hate to think of poor Casper being stuck in doggy limbo."

She leans over and blows out the big white candle, then looks up, her eyes drying. "Right, who's next?" Alexis asks.

Mia and I look at each other. I'm not ready to go just yet. I'm worried it won't work and I'm worried that will hurt too much. Everything has hurt just that bit too much since Aidan broke it off.

Mia must sense my reluctance, as she nods and says, "I'll go next. But I'm a tiny bit scared." She puts her head down and her black hair flops over her face.

"Hey, it's us," I say. "There's no need to be scared." I lean over all the candles in the middle, almost setting myself on fire, and squeeze Mia's knee. "What spell do you want to cast?"

She stays hiding behind her hair for a moment or two more, before she makes herself look up at us. "A binding spell," Mia says. "It's a spell you do to stop someone doing harm ... and I want to cast it on myself." She lifts her chin firmly. "I need to bind myself."

CHAPTER NINE

Mia has had darkness inside her as long as I've known her, since we were only four. I remember being in nursery and Mia arrived, all shy and hiding behind her mum. She sulked in a corner with her teddy bear, clutching the cuddly toy like it was a life raft.

I was very intrigued by this new person, who was so silent compared to the racket of everyone else in nursery. So I picked up another teddy, toddled over and held it out to her.

"Do you want this teddy too?" I asked.

Mia looked up from behind her toy's fur,

examining my offering. Her small hand darted out and took the bear from me, then she hid behind both of them.

I wandered off, feeling proud of myself that she'd accepted my gift.

The next day, Mia got my attention again. She was alone in the sandpit, not using the diggers or the buckets or any of the other cool stuff. Mia was simply sat with her hands stuck in the sand, totally still. I approached her with a spare spade – my second offering.

"Hello," I said, holding out my present. "Do you want to dig with me?" But Mia didn't take it.

Instead, she looked up and said, "Do you think the sand is sad when nobody is playing with it?"

I remember my brain hurting because it had never had a thought like that. Suddenly, I felt so sad for the sand, being left in a box all by itself.

This is the sort of impact Mia has on you.

But I liked it. I liked it so much that I put my spade down, sat next to her and dug my own hands into the sand.

That sums up my friendship with Mia. She has always opened my eyes to things I would have ignored otherwise. "When you play with a certain toy, do you feel sorry for the other toys in case they might feel left out?" she'd ask. "Do you think the moon is jealous of the sun because everyone's asleep when the moon is out?" I'd go around to her chaotic home, with her older brothers and sisters running around everywhere, and she'd take me to her tiny bedroom. There she'd make me write letters to the Queen, asking her to please help save the tigers.

Always earnest, always a bit blue, but always real and always interesting. That's Mia. Together, the two of us became quieter and shyer. We sat reading in corners at primary school, not attracting any attention. I think both of us were glad when Alexis bombarded herself into our friendship group in Year Seven.

"Oh my God," were the first words Alexis said. It was our first day of secondary school and Mia and I were coping with this by sitting in a corner outside, reading. "A spider just fell into my hair," Alexis went on. "MY HAIR! What the hell kind of a school is this? Is it out?"

She shoved her long hair into our startled faces.

"Well, is it?" Alexis demanded. "IS IT?"

We located the spider, which was hard, as Alexis kept screaming and running around and flapping her hands. Then we all lay back laughing and out of breath, and it was as if Alexis had been with us the whole time.

"I'm Alexis," she told us. "How do you two know each other? You act like sisters or something."

"Hi, I'm Sophia. This is Mia. We went to the same primary school."

"Wow, and you actually want to continue hanging out with each other?" Alexis said. "You two must be nice. I've spent all day hiding from everyone I know from primary school."

That's how it came to be. The three of us. One sad, one dramatic, one neutral.

That's me – boring and neutral. Too boring to hold the heart of someone as interesting as Aidan Chambers. Or even the heart of someone who's supposed to love me without question, like Dad. As we've continued at school, I guess our labels have got stronger. Alexis is increasingly dramatic. She's always getting detention for talking too much, and she's always in battles with someone from the other friendship groups she hangs out with.

Alexis sometimes tries to start dramas with

us, but I keep the peace. I have got more boring, I guess. Since Dad left, I've worried so much it was my fault that I've got quieter in case I push people away.

And Mia's sadness went from quirky sad to totally sad. Then, last year, she came in wearing a long-sleeved shirt, even though it was a boiling May day. I teased her about it and she clammed up and told me to shut up. A few months ago, I felt total horror when she pulled her sleeves up in Art without thinking and revealed a criss-cross of bloody scratches across the top of her arms. It was like someone had played multiple games of noughts and crosses on her skin with a compass. It made my stomach fall out and throat close in, as I realised she must have done it to herself.

"What do we do?" Alexis said to me that day when I whispered what I'd seen in the toilets in the English block. "She's so sad. We've got to help her!"

"She's always been sad," I replied.

"Yeah, but never hurting-herself sad."

"I don't know." I shook my head. "Maybe it's a one-off. I don't know why she's doing it. All I know is that I know Mia, and if we try to get her to talk about it, she will shut us out."

She would. She'd push us away and lie or deflect, and I thought it was better to keep Mia close, ready for when she did decide to open up to us.

So it's been a few months now and we've all just sort of pretended it wasn't happening. Mia has just worn long sleeves – that was a given. But now, in this magic circle, Mia is finally talking about it.

CHAPTER TEN

"I've been trying to stop," Mia tells us as the candlelight in the magic circle hits her wet eyes. "I went on this charity website and they gave me all these tips, like holding ice-cubes and snapping an elastic band against my wrist. But it doesn't ever help. I keep doing it ... I know you know I keep doing it."

Alexis and I are frozen. We don't want to stop her now that she's finally talking. I feel like my bedroom is suddenly covered in landmines. If I move, or even speak, I'm going to accidentally set one off and ruin everything.

"So I thought this might help," Mia continues. "Does that sound crazy?"

Alexis and I look at each other.

"It's not crazy at all," I get out. "You know we're always here for you, right?"

Mia wipes her nose and gives a small smile. "I know. You guys have been great about not pushing me on this. Thank you for not telling me off or anything."

Alexis bites on her lower lip. "Are you sure you only want to cast a spell to stop it, though? Like, shouldn't you talk to your parents or your GP or something?"

Mia shakes her head firmly. "No, no way. I don't want anyone to know. I can sort this out by myself."

My stomach twists, like it's trying to wring itself out. I don't feel strong enough to take this on between just the three of us. Worry trickles into my bloodstream. There's a difference between suspecting your friend is doing that to herself and having it confirmed.

"Guys, you're looking at me weird," Mia says. "Stop looking at me weird. This is why I didn't want to tell you."

"Sorry," I say. "I just want you to be OK."

"I'm fine."

But you're clearly not, I think. But I don't say that. "Well, if you're sure ... How do you do a binding spell then?"

Mia seems relieved that she's been let off the hook and brightens. She digs around in her bag and says, "I've got all the ingredients here."

"Did you just say 'ingredients'?" Alexis asks.

Mia gasps, a black candle in one hand. "Oh my God. I did."

The three of us cackle like witches, which I guess we are, at least for tonight. Hearing Mia laugh is like sucking on a throat pastille.

"You guys are the WORST," Mia says. She places a torn-out page of notepad in front of her, along with a pen and a length of black cotton. "How am I supposed to stay a miserable soul-searching type with you two always making me laugh?"

"You love us and you know it," Alexis says.

Mia smiles downwards, wrapping the cotton around one of her fingers. "Yes, well, maybe I do."

Her smile releases the tightness in my stomach and I feel suddenly more able to cope with it all. This is what I love about our friendship group – this ability to share anything. It makes even the hardest stuff feel light enough to carry.

"Can we get back into serious witch mode?" Mia asks. "I do want to take this spell seriously."

"Of course, of course," I say.

Alexis and I both sit up and go silent, while Mia strikes a match and leans over to light the black candle. Her sleeve pulls up and there they are. Fresh scars across her forearm – new and angry looking. Oh, I do hope this spell works. I feel sick looking at Mia's arm. The fact that she'd do that to herself willingly ... it makes no sense at all.

"I just need to write down the name of the person I'm binding on this paper," she says, and writes "Mia Castleton" in her loopy style. I've always been jealous of her handwriting. Once she's done that, she folds the paper up and starts wrapping the black cotton around it.

"I'm binding you, Mia Castleton," she says. "I'm surrounding you with positive energy so you can no longer harm yourself or the people around you. I'm binding you, Mia Castleton."

Mia then holds out the bound paper over the black candle and sets it on fire.

"I bind you, Mia Castleton, I bind you, I bind you," she chants.

I'm not sure whether I should join in or not. To be honest, I don't really want to bind my best friend. I want her to stop hurting herself, but this feels a tad too drastic. And a lot less helpful than speaking to the school counsellor.

I stay silent as the paper bursts into flames, filling my nostrils with the sharp tang of smoke. I hope the smoke alarm doesn't go off.

"Umm, Mia?" Alexis says calmly as the flame grows bigger. "Where are you planning on putting that out?"

"Oh no! I didn't think of that," Mia replies.

The flame's almost reached her hand as I grab my mug of hot orange squash. "Shove it in here," I say.

"I can't put my bound self in hot orange squash!" Mia complains. "Oww, hang on." She drops it into my cup with a giant hiss. I look down into my drink, which is now a grey sludge. It looks like the least magical and grossest thing ever.

"Well, that ruined the atmosphere," Alexis comments. "Nothing like hot orange squash to cramp the witchy vibes."

I think Mia's going to cry then. Her face is pale and pinched, but she doesn't. Instead, thankfully, she bursts out laughing and says, "Well, it's worth a bloody try, isn't it? Maybe the orange squash will even be the secret ingredient."

"Totally won over by the word 'ingredient' now," Alexis says.

We pee ourselves laughing and I think all of us are relieved that the binding is over. Alexis turns to me.

"Right then, Miss Broken Heart," she says.

"It's your turn. I wonder, oh, I wonder, what your spell is going to be about."

CHAPTER ELEVEN

"What's your surname?" Aidan Chambers asked after our third day kissing by the school gates and then going to McDonald's.

His question hurt more than it should. "You don't know my surname?" I said, leaning down and taking a slurp of my milkshake so Aidan couldn't see my face slump.

"No," he said. "Why? Do you know mine?"

Of course I do, I thought. *You are Aidan Chambers. I have practised what my first name sounds like combined with your surname in case we get married. You have to admit that Sophia*

Chambers does sound pretty good, doesn't it?

"Maybe I just remember it from the programme when you were in the school play," I say.

"Aww, you saw me in the school play?"

Twice. I went two nights in a row.

"Err, yeah. I think so. Maybe it was *Carousel*? Was that the one you were in?"

Aidan answered the question by kissing me.

I was pleased that he kept kissing me, because I was really enjoying being kissed by Aidan Chambers. Every moment I wasn't kissing him, I thought about kissing him. I'd go home late, after hours of kissing over strawberry milkshakes, and lie in bed and replay how amazing it felt. I couldn't believe I had such close contact with him. Him. Aidan Chambers. Finally I could ask him all the things I'd spent three years wondering.

"What's your favourite song of all time?"

"Do you believe in God?"

"What's your family like?"

"What's your favourite food?"

I asked between kisses and milkshake sips and Aidan seemed to enjoy answering all those questions. But he never asked any back.

"Who believes in God any more?" he replied. "I really hate my parents, doesn't everyone? Burgers."

It sort of worried me that Aidan didn't seem that interested in getting to know anything other than the inside of my mouth, but I figured I had nothing interesting to share anyway.

Chemistry lessons became vastly more enjoyable than any Chemistry lesson ever should be. As Miss Matthews blahed on about magnesium, Aidan would run his hand up and down my leg under the table. He never went further than the hem of my skirt, but still, I spent every lesson with a face the colour of a raspberry having a violent reaction to another raspberry. And, outside of class, everyone looked at us. The whole school. I went from a total no one to a full-blown celebrity. People *spoke* to me in my other lessons. Some girls started French plaiting their hair. Everyone looked at me, Mia and Alexis in the canteen as we sat where we've always sat, sharing a plate of potato smileys.

"I don't like this," Mia said, shoving one whole into her mouth. "Everyone looking. I feel like I have to wear make-up to school now."

"You wear about ten tons of eyeliner to school every day," I pointed out, taking a bite of my potato smiley so he was just a smile with no eyes. It was true. Mia was always in detention for her make-up.

"Yeah, but now I feel like I have to wear concealer too."

Alexis sat up straighter and fluffed her hair. "I quite like everyone looking."

"Surprise, surprise," Mia said.

"It's funny," Alexis went on. "I feel famous by association. People keep asking me about you in my lessons."

"What?" I said.

"Yeah. I have to tell them what a total bitch you are ... Only joking!"

I looked over at the cause of all the fuss. Aidan Chambers. The boy I was fairly certain I was falling in love with. He was sitting with his usual crowd, chugging a bottle of Diet Coke, laughing manically at a joke Paul Clarrin had just told. My stomach melted. I touched my lips, but I didn't go over. We'd never spoken about it, but, apart from the kissing at the gates and the hand-holding under the Chemistry table, we didn't acknowledge our relationship at school.

I kept pretending it wasn't a problem, but I secretly worried Aidan was ashamed of me or something. Then I'd remind myself he wouldn't kiss me at the gates if he was.

"I don't know why everyone's so fascinated by me," I said, trying to play it cool.

"Are you kidding?" Mia replied, and pulled her sleeves further down. "Whenever Aidan has started seeing someone new, you have got obsessed with them. You start asking me for their freakin' star sign and things."

"What? That was only that one time," I argue. "And I KNEW Gemma Teagan was a Capricorn."

"How about the time you made us stalk Jessica Hadley to check she was really a vegan?" Alexis reminds me.

"We just HAPPENED to be going to town that day anyway. And we just HAPPENED to go into McDonald's at the same time as her. And I

KNEW she was lying about being a vegan. Aidan deserves to be with someone truthful."

I was not happy about Mia and Alexis bringing up all these other past girls. I was trying very hard to block out the fact that, yes, Aidan went through several girls a month. He may have been my very first kiss, but I certainly wasn't his. There had been a kind of carousel pattern to his romantic behaviour, but I was sure the ride was going to stop with me. Aidan and I had a connection. I mean, the day before, he'd squeezed my hand and said, "You ask the funniest questions," when I'd asked him which political party he'd vote for when he was older. I bet he didn't talk politics with his exes. Plus there was the spell I'd cast on the Bunsen burner that kept us together.

I worried about that spell every day.

Why was he with me, if it wasn't because of

that? I was boring; I was beige. I was the sort of girl you didn't notice in a corridor for three years. I was torn in two – half of me totally convinced we were falling in love and would stay together for ever, the other half completely sceptical about Aidan's interest in me.

"I just worry, that's all," Mia said, swallowing another potato smiley. "It's like a circus. I don't want you to get hurt."

I crossed my arms over my chest. "I don't remember asking your advice."

"Oh, come on. Don't be like this."

"Like what?" I demanded.

"All defensive," Mia said. "Look, I'm happy for you. I know you've fancied Aidan for ever. But he's not even come over to say hello. He's not even bothered to introduce himself to me and Lexi. Your best friends! Does that not strike you as weird?"

"It strikes me as weird that you're supposed

to be my friend and therefore supposed to be happy for me."

Alexis's head jerked from one side to the other as she watched us argue, her mouth open. I don't think she'd ever seen me lose my temper.

"I can be happy for you and worried about you at the same time," Mia said.

"Or maybe just jealous of me," I replied.

It was Mia's turn for her mouth to drop open. "You're kidding, right? Jealous?"

"Yes. Jealous ..." I couldn't think of anything else to say to back that up, so I was left with only one option – to flounce off. But where? Then it struck me – maybe I could kill two birds with one stone. So I found myself walking across the canteen towards Aidan Chambers' busy table full of popular people. As I moved, everyone around me parted, like they could foresee the upcoming drama.

This is fine, I told myself. *Aidan likes you. He said as much two days ago when his tongue was in your mouth. It came out more like "IWD LIDET YOUD" because his tongue was very much occupied, but it's the thought that counts. It's fine, totally fine; what you are doing is fine and ...*

I was at his table.

Aidan had been mid-laugh when he sensed me and turned, looking a bit shocked.

This is fine, this is fine, this is fine.

"Oh, hey," was all he said.

"Hey." I crossed my arms around myself, feeling very odd indeed.

"You all right?" he asked.

"Yeah, you?" I replied.

"Yeah, I'm great."

Aidan didn't look or sound great. He seemed unsettled and a tiny bit pissed off. He didn't put his arm around me, or kiss me, or ask me to sit down. He was just looking at me weirdly, like I'd gatecrashed his life. I just had to stand there, with him watching, and all of his friends watching, and my friends I was trying to prove wrong watching, and basically the whole school watching.

I'd made a huge mistake.

Our love only existed outside the school gates, not inside them.

I'd never felt more embarrassed in my whole life.

Nausea swept over me. My hands shook under my jumper sleeves. I had to style it out, while dying over and over on the inside, my heart ripping at the seams. I had no choice but to pretend this wasn't totally horrifically awfully terribly awful.

"Umm, sorry to interrupt," I said to Aidan, my voice casual. "I just wanted to let you know that I'm busy after school today. I forgot to tell you."

I was pretty pleased with that one. I mean, of course I *wasn't* busy after school. I'd literally stopped doing anything after school since Aidan had asked me out. But this was the only way I could think of leaving this situation with any dignity intact.

"Oh," Aidan said. "No worries." He did not look worried at all, to be honest. Whereas I now realised I'd just cancelled our date FOR NO REASON and was devastated.

"No worries," I repeated back at him. Like a stupid twat parrot. "I, er ... have to go to class now or I'll be late."

This was another lie. Lunch did not finish for another twenty minutes. We all knew this.

"Oh, cool, bye," Aidan said. "See you in Chemistry."

I stood there, blinking. Waiting for him to kiss me. Not even a proper kiss, but at least a small peck, one to reassure me that I hadn't dreamed every afternoon for the last two weeks. But Aidan just waved his hand, like I was a departing grandma who'd come to stay for the weekend. Then he turned back to his mates as if nothing had happened. While I fled from the canteen and burst into tears in the English-block loos.

"Don't say I told you so," I yelled through my tears when Mia and Alexis found me.

"Are you OK?" Mia called down as her head appeared over the top of my stall. "Let us in."

"I mean, I could be pooing in here," I went on. "You can't just go around poking your head over the tops of cubicles."

"We actually did see a girl pooing just now when we checked the Art block," Alexis said, her head bobbing up next to Mia's. "Poor little

Year Seven. I think she'll be traumatised for life."

I couldn't even laugh. I just cried harder, scrambling up to let Mia and Alexis into my cubicle. We all crammed inside and they hugged me hard and said, "There, there."

"I'm so embarrassed," I said.

"Don't be, no one saw," Mia said.

"Apart from everyone in the canteen," Alexis pointed out.

"I don't understand ..." I sat back on the closed loo seat and folded my face onto my knees. "I mean, Aidan and I are together, aren't we? Why is what I did so strange? Why did he behave so strangely? I'm so confused."

"You are not the only one who is confused," Mia said. "But I'm mainly confused about why you fancy such an arsehole who doesn't acknowledge you in public."

"He does!" I argued. "At the school gates!"

"And just now?"

"I don't know what just happened. I shouldn't have ... have ... broken the terms of our relationship."

At this, Alexis and Mia both squatted down so they were at my eye level and looked at me with serious faces. "Honey," Alexis said. "I'm sorry to say this, but I don't think you're in a relationship."

I didn't want to believe them, of course. I told them thank you, but you are wrong. Thank you, but it was a misunderstanding. Thank you, but I'm sure Aidan and I will figure it out. Thank you, and I will forgive you in time for our wedding, don't worry.

I kept my head down for the rest of the afternoon. I got all my work done in lessons. I used my hair as a shield against the world. I agreed to go to town with the girls so I had something to do later rather than sitting at home feeling embarrassed. Then we were going to go to Alexis's and do face masks because she'd heard the sheet ones were on offer at Superdrug. I felt a bit better as Mia, Alexis and I linked arms to leave school and walk home via town. I could kiss Aidan Chambers at the school gates tomorrow. I'd get it back to how it was. I'd just rushed him, that was all. He was just a bit scared by the intensity of his feelings.

It was cold and everyone's breaths came out as puffs of white that floated up into the freezing afternoon sky. Alexis picked up a twig and pretended to smoke and I howled with laughter – feeling better and glad for my friends. Then Alexis paused, twig still in her mouth.

"Oh, Sophia," she said.

I ground to a halt just before we got to the school gates.

"What?" I asked. "What is it?"

But my heart already knew.

I followed Alexis's gaze. Aidan Chambers was at the gates, as always. But not as always. Because he wasn't kissing me. He was kissing that Capricorn cowbag, Gemma Teagan.

CHAPTER TWELVE

I pull out one white candle and one red candle from where they've been hiding under my bed, and the cheap dying red rose that Mia brought.

"Isn't it, like, unethical to cast a love spell on someone?" Alexis asks.

Her nose wrinkles as I also get out a photo of me and Aidan. I printed it this morning. It's the only photo I have of us. One I took in McDonald's. Both sipping from straws in the same milkshake. The only evidence that we've shared anything at all.

I get out the final ingredient – a long length

of silk I'd bought in town. "I was googling it earlier to check and it's fine," I reply. "This isn't going to interfere with Aidan's free will or anything. It's just putting energy out into the universe to remind him of his love for me."

Mia shakes her head. "If he needs to be reminded of it, then it's not love, babe."

"Come on. I was serious about your spells. I've just helped a freakin' dog cross over to the other side."

Mia holds up her hands. "I'm just saying."

I put the photo down, with Aidan's gorgeous eyes staring up at me. "Look," I say, "I admit that his behaviour has not been perfect. I'm not denying that. In my ideal world, no, I would not have to cast a spell to get my boyfriend to remember he likes me. But we are not living in an ideal world and I just want to put something out into the universe to help him along. I'm just trying to remind Aidan that he thinks I'm great. What. Is. Wrong. With. That?"

Alexis is smiling. "You're so cute when you're angry."

"Stop it."

"What?"

"Making fun of me."

"I'm not!" Alexis complains. "We don't see you like this very much, that's all. All angry. It's funny."

"Can we just get on with the spell already?" I say.

I close my eyes and try to get myself into the magic zone – a bit like the trance I was in when I cast the spell on the Bunsen burner. Intention is the most important ingredient in magic. You have to believe your spell will work. You can't have doubts or the universe will pick up on them and ruin things. I picture the grand reconciliation between Aidan and me. I see us kissing at the school gates again, but I want to add to the fantasy to feed it and let the universe know how seriously I'm taking this. So I picture Aidan introducing me to all his friends as his girlfriend, and reserving me a seat in the front row of the next school play, and coming to pick me up for the Year Eleven prom, where we win King and Queen, even though that's two years away. I'm just picturing my prom dress – green with lace, maybe – when something hits my head.

I open my eyes. "Oww," I say. Alexis has balled up the silk and thrown it at me.

"We needed to get your attention," she says.

"Are you finished laughing at me?" I ask.

They both sigh. "We weren't laughing at you," Mia says. "We *love* you. You never need to cast a spell on us, for example."

"Yes, yes, yes. I see your point. Can we just get started?"

I get us to link hands and try to get my brain back into a witchy place. I take some deep breaths and try to feel connected to the universe.

"Mother Nature," I say, feeling very self-conscious, "I call on you to help bring love back into my life. I ask that you help lost affection find its way again. First, I appoint this silk with flame." I light the red and the white candles I've bought and hold the silk above the flames for a moment, but not so long that it burns. Then I take the picture of Aidan and me and rip it in half down the middle. I hand both pieces to Mia. "I've got to close my eyes for the next bit," I tell her. "When I say so, can you pass me the photo of Aidan?"

Mia nods and takes the ripped photo, and I'm pleased neither of them are taking the piss any more. They're letting me focus on the spell.

I close my eyes into darkness and lift up the warmed silk. "Mother Nature, here is silk, touched by the flame of love. I ask that you bind with it all the lost feelings of love, affection and acceptance."

I hold out my hand. "Mia," I whisper, "the photo."

"Oh yeah, here it is."

I fumble for Mia's hand and pluck the Aidan photo from her. Then, with my eyes still closed, I fold the photo and wrap the silk around it till it's fully covered. "And now, Mother Nature," I say, "I will plant this and the rose at the bottom of a tree, so the love can take root and grow from a place of strength. Thank you, and thanks to all the spirits as well."

"Thank you," Mia repeats.

"Cheers, dudes," Alexis says.

"And that's it." I open my eyes to find Alexis and Mia both grinning at me.

"Now what?" Alexis asks.

"We just need to bury his photo."

"Outside?"

"Yes."

"Ergh. But it's so cold!" Alexis crosses her arms.

"Final hurdle, guys, come on," I say.

I stand up, the silk and rose clutched in my hand. Mia gets up slowly, but Alexis has to be dragged up by both hands. We head downstairs, wrap ourselves in hats and gloves and step out into the cold blackness of my back garden.

"This level of coldness is ridiculous," Alexis complains as I plod across the wet grass to our one and only tree. It's a birch tree, glowing silver in the moonlight. Earlier I left a trowel out here and I crouch down to pick it up.

"Will you hold up the light from your phone while I dig?" I ask Mia as I squat down with the silk bundle and rose offering. I start attacking the cold ground. "Yikes. The soil is proper hard."

The two of them protect me from the wind as I struggle to dig a suitable hole. The ground is frozen almost solid and I've never had good upper-body strength. But I'm determined and I manage to dig a tiny hole. Then I drop Aidan's silk-wrapped photo and the rose into it and cover them with earth.

"A cat could dig it up," Mia points out as I'm patting the soil down.

"Nah," I reply. "My mum puts fox wee around the perimeter of our garden so we don't get cats."

Mia pulls a face. "Where the holy hell does she get fox wee from?"

I shrug. "In a bottle from the garden centre."

I give one final pat and stand up. "It's not like she runs after foxes collecting it with a pot or something. That would be weird. Right, that's it. So maybe in a week or two the spell will—"

We all jump as my phone rings.

CHAPTER THIRTEEN

"Oh my God, it's him, it's him," Alexis squeals over the angry shrill of my ringing phone. "The spell worked!"

My heart floats up into my chest and my fingers start shaking, and not just because of the cold. No, it can't have worked. Not that fast. No. No. No.

I look down at my phone.

No.

"Hi, Mum, what's up?" I say, making a face at Mia and Alexis. They start laughing, their breath coming out in big puffs.

"Oh, hi, darling," Mum says. "Sorry to bother you but I'm having an actual panic I left the straighteners on."

I sigh and start trudging back to the house, beckoning for the girls to follow me inside. "Why didn't you just message?"

"Because you wouldn't reply and then I'd worry that you hadn't seen the message and you would all burn to death as you slept."

I roll my eyes. "We have a smoke alarm, Mum." I open up the sliding door into the warm, central-heated air.

"I'm hardly going to rely on that to keep you and your friends alive."

I kick off my shoes so I don't get mud on the carpet and pad upstairs to her room while Mia and Alexis help themselves to more hot squash. Mum's bedroom is always messier than mine and tonight it's particularly bad. She clearly couldn't decide what to wear to her date, as there's an assortment of clothes littering the bed in piles, and high heels kicked off everywhere. "Mum, you are so messy."

"I know, I know. Can you see the straighteners? Are they switched off?"

I scan the cluttered carpet and find them on the heatproof mat, not turned on. I roll my eyes again but then feel instantly guilty. Before Dad left, he was always going on at Mum for "being too stressed". I mean, she is too stressed, but she was even more stressed when Dad was here, constantly telling her how stressed she was. "They're off," I tell Mum. "We will live through the night after all. You can relax."

"Thanks, love," she says. "Are they unplugged at the wall?"

"No."

"Do you mind?"

I sigh again and yank the plug out. It clatters to the carpet.

"Cheers, darling. Sorry, I'll leave you alone now. Have a good time."

I'm about to ask Mum how her evening is going, but then I realise I'm not sure I want to know.

"You too," I say, before hanging up.

I hear Mia and Alexis banging up the stairs and I emerge from Mum's room to find them carrying up giant tubes of crisps alongside their steaming mugs.

"How?" I ask Alexis as we head back into my room.

"All that magic made me hungry," she says. "Plus, you know, it's the—"

"The grief," I interrupt. "Yes, I know."

Mia seems lifted by our magic circle already. She's bouncing on her toes, brimming with energy. She's never normally like this.

"I've downloaded loads of witch movies," Mia says. "We can marathon the whole night. Stopping at midnight of course to go bless the Super Blood Wolf Moon."

"Of course." Alexis rips the lid off some salt and vinegar Pringles and folds two into her mouth.

"So we've got *The Craft* and one called *Practical Magic* and all of *Sabrina*. I've downloaded all of them, so we have a choice. And there's this empowerment spell I found too—"

She's cut off by my phone buzzing in my hand.

"Is it?" Alexis says.

"My mum again?" I answer. "Probably. She'll want me to check I've not left the gas on or something."

I unlock my screen, expecting to see "Mum" flashing up and further instructions about the house. But it isn't her.

"Oh my GOD, guys," I scream. My phone thuds to the carpet as I jump and start flapping my hands.

"What? What is it?" Mia asks.

"It's worked, it's worked, it's worked," I say. "We're witches, we are actually goddamned witches. I knew it, I knew it, I knew it."

Alexis bends down and reads the message out, her voice high and questioning.

Aidan Chambers: Hey, how are things? I'm at Lucy's party. You should come. It would be nice to see u X

CHAPTER FOURTEEN

Alexis has my phone in her hand, her mouth hanging open, shaking her head. Mia leans over, reading the message to check it's true, and her mouth drops open too. Meanwhile I'm running around my bedroom, jumping on the bed like a hyperactive child.

"We're witches, we're witches, we're witches! Guys, WE ARE WITCHES."

"I can't believe it," Mia says. "It could just be a coincidence."

I shake my head as I bounce, bumping my head on the ceiling.

"No way!" I say. "Aidan hasn't messaged me in WEEKS, and now, right after the spell, came the message. Oww!"

"But it can't be ..." Mia begins.

I grab her hands, pull her up onto the bed with me and force her to jump. "Come on, Alexis," I call down.

She grins and climbs up to join us, letting the excitement of what we've just achieved sink in.

"I'm a witch, I'm a witch, I'm a ... OWW," I yelp as I jump too high again and my head collides with the ceiling. I drop to the bed in a lump. "Oww, oww, oww."

The others carry on jumping around me.

"Seriously, guys, stop jumping, it really hurts." I huddle in a ball, tears pricking my eyes at the pain. Alexis and Mia realise I'm not joking and squat down to check on me. Mia reaches out to where I'm cradling my head.

"Yikes, you've actually got a huge lump already," she says.

"Oww."

"Yes, oww," Mia says sympathetically. "It looks oww."

I feel my head and, yep, there's a giant lump forming, like the ones in cartoons. I get a sudden memory of my dad and what he'd always say when I bumped my head as a kid. "Oh no, has somebody's head laid an egg?" Dad's rough hands would gently stroke my lump as I cried. "I didn't know you were a chicken," he'd say.

Then Dad would cluck and do a chicken impression, while I protested, "I'm not a chicken, Daddy!" I'd end up laughing so hard I forgot all about the egg on my head.

Dad could be nice sometimes, I guess ...

Anyway, now is not the time to think about the past, or to have my head grow an egg. No.

I have just cast another successful spell on Aidan Chambers. It turns out that, yes, I do have proper magical powers. Now I need to go find Aidan, follow this magic through, get back together and feel happy again.

I lurch to my feet and run to my wardrobe. "Right, what the hell should I wear to this party?" I yank out some clothes.

"Hang on, we're going to a party?" Mia asks as she slides off the bed, watching me.

"OF COURSE we're going to the party." I pull out a white summer dress made of thin cotton and wonder if I'll get frostbite if I wear it. "Aidan just invited me to the party, so I must go. He never used to invite me to *anything*! This is a breakthrough. A magical breakthrough!"

"But I thought tonight was a girl's night?" Mia's voice is sharp and I see her face turning sour as I glance at her in my mirror.

115

I twist my head back to look at Mia properly. "It was a witch night, to cast spells, and the spells have led us to the party. We have to follow the guidance of Mother Nature."

Alexis looks much more excited. "Plus we NEVER get invited to parties," she says. "This is brilliant." Alexis starts rummaging in my make-up bag. "Can I borrow your lipstick?" she asks, plucking one out. "I didn't bring any. I need to get this eyeliner off too."

"Sure, sure," I reply, nodding while pulling out another unsuitable dress.

Mia crosses her arms and stares at us with a very stinky stink-eye. "I can't believe you're making us go to a party! Tonight was supposed to be a night for just us. You're doing it again. Dumping us the moment Aidan is interested."

"What?" I say, and twist around holding a yellow sundress. "Where the hell did that come from? I never dumped you. And I'm not dumping you now. You can come too!"

"Oh, and watch you lose all your self-respect," Mia replies, "hanging off some guy who doesn't even acknowledge you? Yay! Fun for me! What a way to spend my Saturday night!"

My mouth couldn't be more open. "What the hell? Mia!"

"Yeah, come on, Mia," Alexis says. "That's not fair."

Mia turns to Alexis, her eyes darting and angry. "So you think it's a good idea for Sophia to get back together with Aidan? After what he did?"

Alexis shrugs. "I think it's a good idea for Sophia to do what she wants to do."

"You're ridiculous," Mia says. "You're only saying this because *you* want to go to the stupid party. You're a bad friend!"

"Are you being serious? Honestly?" Alexis replies, and takes a step forward, squaring up to Mia. "You're being totally unreasonable, as always."

"Me?!" Mia shouts. "Unreasonable? You're the one crying over a dog you didn't even like."

I wave my hands in the air to try to stop them. "Guys," I say. "Come on, GUYS."

"I DID LIKE CASPER," Alexis yells. "I LOVED HIM. HOW DARE YOU?"

Mia crosses her arms further, her jaw jutting out. "You *hated* that dog. You talked about how much you hated him all the time."

"Guys!" I say.

"Well, you hate everyone and everything!" screams Alexis. "You're, like, INCAPABLE of being happy. It's so boring."

"GUYS!" I repeat, then step so I'm between them. Mia's face is all pinched. She turns away and starts shoving all her sleepover stuff back into her rucksack.

"Well, if you're going to be like that," Mia says.

"Mia, come on," I say. "Don't go."

I'm feeling too many emotions. I'm so elated about Aidan's message. It's as if my heart has sprung loose from its chest and is jittering all around my body with excitement and nerves and joy. But now I'm freaking out about Mia. What is going on with her tonight? Why is she being so mean? She can't leave! What if she hurts herself? I watch Mia pack and feel a final emotion that I'm almost ashamed to admit ... annoyance. Why does she always have to make everything about her? It's not fair that I can't enjoy myself without always worrying about her. "Come on, Mia," I plead. "Let's not all fight."

"I'm not fighting. I just don't want to go to this stupid party."

Alexis has her arms crossed too and she's staring sulkily at the Pringles. "If you don't want to come, then don't come."

"Alexis!" I say.

"What?" she replies. "There's no point dragging Mia there."

I make mad eyes at Alexis. Has she not realised the danger here? Mia just admitted to us that she self-harms – we can't leave her alone after something like that! But Alexis just walks past me to my wardrobe. "Do you have any clothes I can borrow?" she asks me, opening the doors and rummaging inside. "Your black top? Or are you wearing it?"

I ignore her and step towards Mia.

"Come just for an hour, Mia," I plead. "Please."

"You don't need me there anyway," Mia says. She keeps shaking her head and won't look at me. "You'll just jump on Aidan the moment you arrive and we'll have to watch you guys make out and pretend we don't think he's an arsehole."

"Please come," I repeat, "and stop calling him an arsehole."

"No."

"Mia, come on."

We can't leave her on her own. But I also can't not go to the party now that I've summoned Aidan back. That will just confuse the spirits. I squeeze my hands into fists, wishing I could cast a spell to make Mia less difficult.

"Can't we just stay here?" she asks, finally looking up, her eyes wet. "You know the party will be terrible. Nobody knows us or likes us."

Alexis is already down to her bra and yanking one of my tops over her head. "Because they've not had the chance to!" Alexis says. "This will give them the chance." She wiggles into the top and I get a pang of jealousy that she looks better in it than I do.

"So our friendship group isn't enough for you?" Mia says. "Is that it?"

I raise my hands before Alexis can reply. "Hey, hey, hey. Mia, where is all this coming from?" I make my voice as low and as calm as I can, and it works. She tears up, sniffs and says, "Sorry. I just ... feel weird about everything I shared tonight, and now I'm scared that you guys don't want to be friends with me."

Alexis and I look at each other and both of us soften, forgiving Mia straight away now her behaviour makes sense. We run to Mia's side and sit her on the bed.

"Mia, that is just mental," I say. "Of COURSE we still want to be your friend."

"These things have nothing to do with one another," Alexis adds. "Sophia can love you and be glad and relieved that you shared that with us but also want to go to this party."

I feel Mia relax into our hug as our words soothe her. "Fine then, I'll go," she says, resting her head on me. "Even though I don't want to."

"Yes!" I say.

"It will be terrible," Mia warns. "And we'll probably all end up crying."

Alexis leaps up and starts doing a crazy dance move, looking like she's fighting with a chicken. "But we'll be LIVING," she says, her arms flying out in a frenzy. "Crying, but living."

Alexis carries on dancing like a nutcase, making us all laugh, even Mia. Then I get to work removing the eyeliner from my face. I cannot win back the love of my life while made up to scare children. I open a packet of wet wipes and smear the eyeliner off my face, then start applying more mascara.

My spell. It worked. He messaged. He actually messaged. I love him. I do think I love him. Is this the start of him loving me? Of someone finally loving me?

"I'm not changing," Mia says as she watches us preen ourselves into oblivion. She pulls her hoodie sleeves down, picks up a book and starts reading it against the wall while she waits for us. I grin. I love how we can have epic rows that take us right to the edge of our friendship and then switch right back into all being best friends again. It shows how safe we are with each other. I always see our arguments as a sign of strength rather than weakness.

I examine my face in the mirror to see if my giant eyelashes are fluttery enough. My mouth is doing this weird thing where it can't stop smiling.

I apply a peach lipstick, one that makes

the blue in my eyes really stand out. One that doesn't smear. Just in case.

I wonder what Aidan Chambers is wearing.

I wonder how many times he's checked his phone to see if I've replied.

I wonder if I should start saving now for our limo to the Year Eleven ball.

I wonder if the only reason he's messaged is because I cast a spell on him.

I hope not. I really hope not. But I do worry.

CHAPTER FIFTEEN

There was a moment where I considered how far
I could go in my life with no Chemistry GCSE.
I mean, the THOUGHT of having to sit next to
Aidan for two hours every week, learning about
the periodic bloody table, after he'd broken my
heart and peed on its shattered pieces was just
impossible.

I cried solidly the weekend after it
happened – looking at the one photo I had
of us on my phone over and over. It wasn't
just the hurt of Aidan rejecting me but the
humiliation I felt that everyone knew about it.

Public confirmation that, yes, I *was* unlovable, undesirable, boring and bland. Mum didn't know what to do with the crying mess that was me. She thought it was something to do with Dad leaving, even though it had been several months since he'd taken off.

"Oh, hon, I'm sorry," Mum soothed. "It wasn't your fault he left. He was just a very confused man. It was nothing to do with you – you're perfect."

I cried harder, as being reminded of my dad upping and leaving to freaking Canada was also a painful thing to think about.

She sat on the edge of my bed and brushed my hair clumped with tears off my forehead. "Honey, never think it's about you. Your dad loves you, in his own way. He just ... well ... he loves himself more. But that's his issue, not yours."

I turned away from Mum without saying anything and wondered instead how I could permanently avoid Chemistry. Maybe if I did really badly I could get put down a set? Except part of me was still desperate to see Aidan, as pathetic as that sounds. Maybe he'd realise his mistake when he saw me? Maybe ... maybe ...

It was ridiculous how dressed up I got for school on the Tuesday. I really pushed the boundaries of the make-up rules and how far I could roll up my skirt.

"You look lovely," Alexis told me during form time as she passed me some gum. "He never deserved you, you know that, right?"

"Who?" I replied. "What? Oh, him. Not even thought about it."

"No? So these messages weren't from you

over the weekend?" She pulled out her phone, coughed and started whispering out loud.

"'I will never feel joy again.'"

"'It's my left eye, isn't it? He didn't like the fact it's smaller than my right eye.'"

"'I've cried so hard that I think my face has had an allergic reaction.'"

"Stop it!" I went to snatch her phone off her while she cracked up. "I get your point."

Before the Chemistry lesson I stood in the English-block bathroom, rehearsing my *I don't care about you at all and I'm handling this so maturely* face. It involved a lot of relaxed eyebrows.

"You can do this," I told my reflection. "Show Aidan what he's missing. Show him that you're NOT boring and you're NOT bland and you're totally amazing and he's an idiot to be kissing Gemma instead of you."

Aidan was already sitting down when I made my way into Chemistry. My insides melted at the sight of him. God, he was so good looking. It really shouldn't be allowed. There should be some kind of law where boys over a certain level of attractiveness should be forced to wear paper bags over their heads. It wasn't fair on anyone really.

Every step towards Aidan was hard. I noticed most of the class looking at me, wondering how this was going to play out. It was my last snatch of being interesting to my year group before I drifted back to being a nobody again.

I got to my seat. Aidan looked up.

"Oh, hey," he said, like nothing was the matter at all. "You good?"

Why is he pretending nothing has happened?

Has nothing happened? Did I hallucinate the whole thing? Am I about to be transported back to the day I cast the love spell over the Bunsen burner, shaking myself awake and realising the whole thing was just a daydream, warning me of the perils of magic?

"Me? Oh yeah, I'm so good," I found myself replying. "Gooder than a … a goody two shoes. I'm like … umm … a goody ten shoes."

Aidan smirked like I was a weirdo. "Cool."

I sat down. "Are you, like, also good?"

"Yeah, I'm *great*."

That *great* hurt me the most. It was very impressive I didn't cry right there and then. Instead, I sat next to Aidan, unravelling. I hung my hair over my face so he couldn't look at me. Not that he tried to look at me anyway. He didn't even talk to me. He didn't try to offer an explanation for what had happened. Aidan just took notes and listened to the teacher and left with a simple "Bye then" when the bell rang.

And I went home and cried and wondered what was wrong with me. First my dad, leaving me like it was absolutely nothing. No big deal. It wasn't like he was MY FATHER or anything. And now Aidan Chambers. My first kiss. Also exiting my life like it was no big deal. Like I was no big deal ...

CHAPTER SIXTEEN

It doesn't matter how hard you put together the perfect party look, it will always get ruined by the many layers needed to survive the British winter.

"You would never know how good my boobs look under all this," Alexis complains as we stomp over the frost towards Lucy's party. Alexis is swaddled in two scarves, a hat and a giant puffer jacket. "And they're extra firm because of the cold."

I see Mia roll her eyes as we walk under the orange glow of a streetlight. "We're hardly going to bump into the loves of our lives walking in the suburbs on our way to a crap party," she says.

"You never know!" Alexis replies.

I'm not concentrating properly on their conversation because I am very, very nervous indeed. I've messaged Aidan back with a very breezy, "Oh, I am free tonight after all, maybe I'll come down." I've been checking my phone every twenty seconds since. No reply yet. But maybe that's because he's giving himself a talking-to in the mirror. I picture people lining up outside Lucy's bathroom while Aidan has locked himself in. He's gripping the sink, looking at himself and saying, "Don't screw this up, mate; this is your one shot to win Sophia back."

I stop for a second, skidding on the ice, as it hits me that I know deep down that this isn't happening. Not even with my spell. Aidan Chambers would never care that much.

"How long do we have to stay at the party?" Mia whinges as she skids on the same patch of ice I just did.

"At least one whole hour," Alexis says. "And you have to talk to one whole human who isn't us."

"This is going to be terrible," Mia complains.

"No, it's not," Alexis replies. "Have you not been following the hashtag?"

"No. What hashtag?"

It turns out that Lucy has made a hashtag for the party – #WinterBall – and we all slide to a halt to check it out on Alexis's phone. Anyone who is anyone from school seems to be there, posting selfies and full-length photos of their outfits. Someone's managed to get hold of loads of alcohol, as everyone's holding beer bottles or wine glasses. We scroll over more photos and I keep my eye out for Aidan, my stomach tight with nerves, ready and waiting for sight of the boy who asked me to come.

"Looks like Peter and Olivia are back together," Alexis is saying. "If the solid kissing is anything to go by. Oh my God, is that Ryan? I've not seen him since he was expelled."

More photos flick past, but I can sense Mia getting cold and bored next to me.

"Where the hell did they get all that wine from?" Alexis muses. "It MUST be Charlie's dad's, but surely his parents would notice … oh."

That's when his face appears. Aidan Chambers' perfect face. I grab Alexis's phone off her.

"Hey," she says, but I ignore her.

Aidan looks good, of course. Hair all sticky-uppy. A nice checked shirt on. Skin with its year-round natural tan. Teeth looking all white against it. He's got a beer in one hand and is doing the peace sign with the other. He looks so beautiful. My stomach turns cartwheels. God, I fancy him. I can't *believe* he messaged me. Me? Me! Me. *But ... but ...* a voice in my head starts to whisper. *But ...*

"Can I have my phone back?" Alexis asks. "Earth to Sophia! Phone. Mine. Can I have it back?"

"Oh, sorry." I hand it over and we start walking again, but I'm looking down at the frosty pavement and my stomach is doing something I don't understand. It's not fizzing any more. The cartwheels have turned into belly flops. In fact, my stomach feels like a blodge of something un-good. Dread has crept into my intestines. No, it can't be that. My wish has come true. My spell has worked.

Blodge.

There it goes again.

What's happening?

I skid to yet another halt and my friends slide next to me, their legs Bambi-ing under them.

"What is it?" Mia asks. "You OK?"

I nod, staying still. "No."

"That's a confusing response," Mia says.

I shake my head. "Yes, sorry."

"That's even more confusing."

"Sorry." I watch my breath come out in puffs. And I'm not sure where all this blodge is coming from, or what's going on, or why I'm suddenly thinking about my dad, and how he left, and how that made my tummy hurt too. And now I'm thinking about Aidan Chambers, and what he did, and how that made me feel.

"I'm ... I'm not sure if I want to go," I find myself saying out loud. I grab my throat, surprised at what I've just said.

"You're kidding, right?" Alexis says, while I see Mia smile to the side of us.

I shake my head once more. "I don't know. I'm confused."

"We're all dressed up," Alexis adds. "We're ready. He's messaged you! This is everything you wished for."

"But is it?" I ask, and I touch my throat again, shocked at the words it has just produced. Words that I never imagined I'd ever say. But the words feel right. They tingle on my tongue as I say them.

"If you don't want to go, we don't have to go," Mia says.

Alexis twists to her. "Oh, don't pretend you're not delighted."

"I just want what's best for Sophia."

"So do I," Alexis replies, "and she's literally just cast an actual magic spell to get this guy, so I figured she'd want to follow through. Considering magic is a pretty drastic life option and all."

I'm sniffing. A lot actually. I reach a gloved hand up to my nose and it's covered in snot when I pull it away. That's weird. I sniff again, to try to snort up the snot. The noise pulls Alexis and Mia out from their bickering.

"Oh my God, Sophia, what's wrong?" Alexis asks.

"What do you mean?"

"You're crying," Mia says, and steps forward to rub my freezing arms over my coat.

"I ... am?"

They both nod. I put my gloves to my eyes and they come away soggy with both snot and tear juice. I hiccup a sob. God, I really am crying. Woah.

"Bloody hell, I've never seen you cry this hard," Alexis says to me. "Are you OK?"

More tears come in response. They're pouring and pouring now and my chest is starting to hurt.

"Do you mind if we sit down?" I say, and sit very abruptly on the freezing cold pavement. My face collapses into my hands and I cry and cry and cry. My back heaves, snot decorating my knees like there's been a slug orgy.

It all comes out. All of it. I'm crying because I'm realising how stupid I am. I'm crying because Aidan Chambers wasn't very nice to me. In fact, he humiliated me in public and hasn't even said sorry. Just like my dad upped and left us and hasn't once said sorry. I'm crying because these things hurt. I've been pretending I'm OK, but I'm not. It all really, really hurts.

"Am I just nothing?" I wail out into the darkness. "Do I mean nothing to nobody?"

"What?" Alexis says. "Hon. You're amazing."

Both my friends sit next to me and Alexis pulls me in for a hug.

"No, I'm not," I tell her. "I'm boring and pointless and nobody loves me." My voice comes out like a pig just stubbed its trotter. The words, and what they mean, hurt to say out loud and they're letting my emotions run riot.

I blame myself for Dad leaving, I think, *because, surely if I was worth anything, he would've stayed? And then Aidan Chambers came along, giving me hope I was worth something, deserving of time and attention, but then he just got bored too.*

"What makes me so easy to leave?" I sob. "I must be so spectacularly boring if I can be chucked aside just like that."

There's nothing Mia and Alexis can do to stop my tears for a while. So they sit there, in the cold and dark, missing the coolest party we've ever been invited to, and rub my back. There's never one moment where one of them isn't rubbing me, whether it's my back, or my arm, or my cold, cold leg. They rub and rub, like I'm a magic lamp that can grant them wishes, while whispering kindness in my frozen ears.

"Sophia, we love you," Mia says. "You're not boring. You're the most amazing person ever."

"Please don't assume having loads of drama is good," Alexis says. "It's exhausting. I love having you around. You're my rock. That's not nothing; that's everything."

"You shouldn't let him get to you like that."

"He's a dick."

"I'm so sorry about your dad."

I cry until nothing is left and there is absolutely no feeling in either of my butt cheeks. I cry in a way that releases something. I cry at being held by my friends, and I cry at how good that can feel.

And then something magical happens ... I start to believe their words. These reassurances from my friends. They sink in as my tears sink into the frost beneath us. Because I may not be the most zingy of people. I may be someone who listens more than she talks. I may not hold the room, but I hold others up. I keep the peace. I'm there. If I love you, I am there. Even if you're crying about a dead dog you never liked that much. Or making me promise to hold dark scary secrets about what you do to yourself. Or even repeatedly asking me to check your hair straighteners are turned off. I'm there.

Being reliable isn't always boring, I realise. I wish Dad had been more reliable. I wish Aidan had too ... I always saw my reliability as a curse, but now I'm feeling like it could be my strength.

"Thank you," I say eventually, when I'm all out of tears. "I don't know where that came from."

Mia laughs. "Well, now we've each had at least one cry tonight. Well done for equalising."

"Am I mental for not going to the party?" I ask.

They both say no at once and shake their heads wildly like dogs drying themselves off.

"You'd be mental for giving Aidan the time of day," Mia says.

"But he's asked me to come. Surely that must mean something?"

"He's hurt you before," Alexis says. "That should mean something. Much as I want to go to this party, I don't want you to get hurt. And that boy has a pattern."

I shake my head now. "I literally don't understand myself right at this moment. I mean, I cast this spell to get Aidan back and now I—"

I'm cut off by Alexis squeezing my arm. "Oh my God," she squeals. "Guys! It's Casper."

Of all the interruptions in all the world, I was not expecting this one.

"What?" Mia asks.

We follow where Alexis is pointing and our eyes land on a very small, very lost-looking dog. It has to be said, the little thing looks exactly like Alexis's recently deceased Casper.

Alexis jumps up. "It's Casper! He's here to say goodbye." She skids over the road at top speed and is at the animal's side within seconds, crouching down and rubbing the dog behind his ears. "Here, here, boy. Oh my God, I MISS you SO MUCH. I can't believe you came."

Mia and I look at each other. I'm in total shock. Too many spells are coming true. I'm willing to accept Aidan's message as coincidence ... but a resurrected animal?

"That's not her dog, right?" I ask Mia. "It can't be Casper."

Mia smiles. "At this point in the evening, I'm willing to believe anything."

We get up slowly, shell-shocked, and drag our cold bodies over to Jesus-Casper and a now-crying Alexis.

"He's come to say goodbye before he crosses over," Alexis says. She runs her hands through his fur, tears pouring from her eyes. Jesus-Casper is loving it and rolls over so we can get to his stomach. His little legs start twitching with joy as Alexis rubs him. I never, ever saw her be this nice to her dog when he was alive.

"I miss you so much," Alexis says. "I'm sorry I wasn't very nice to you. I hope you have a lovely time in doggy heaven."

I reach my hand out towards the dog's head, almost expecting my hand to pass through him like a ghost. But I make contact with fur and Jesus-Casper leans happily into my hand.

"So weird," I mutter.

Alexis is a transformed person. Not one part of her seems freaked out. She can't stop rubbing the dog. She's the happiest I think I've ever seen her. A smile creeps over my face. I don't know if this Jesus-Casper is actually Casper coming to say goodbye. Maybe it's a coincidence, maybe it's a lost dog, or maybe it's magic. Whatever it is, I'm very glad it's happened.

We all crowd around, rubbing Jesus-Casper for a minute or two. The dog's still on his back, paws up, tongue lolling in pleasure. His eyes stare right at us, like he's telling us, "Please never stop doing this." It's a very real dog. Unless we're all having the same hallucination at once – which is possible as we ate a lot of cheesy pizza – this dog is real. Then, as quickly as he arrived, Jesus-Casper lets out a sharp bark, rolls over and runs off into the darkness. We stand and watch him fade into black.

"Goodbye, Casper," Alexis whispers through tears. "I love you."

I keep shaking my head. "I can't believe we magicked the dog," I say. "First Aidan messaging, then Casper coming back."

Mia puts her hand up. "Orrrrr, maybe that dog was just a lost dog and we've let him run out into the night where he might get eaten by a fox."

"No, that was definitely Casper." Alexis turns to us, smiling the biggest smile the universe has ever seen. "We did it. We helped him cross over. We really do have powers."

We grin at one another and a breeze comes out of nowhere, lifting our hair, chilling us to the bone. We burst out laughing, then sort of scream, giddily frightened. We start running back in the direction of my house, shrieking and stopping occasionally to howl at the blood moon.

We must look like complete nutters, but I feel so much lighter since my cry.

I stop in my front garden and throw my head back to howl again. I marvel at how full I feel when I'm with these girls. How lucky I am that I've met my crazy friends. I don't know why I worry about being unlovable when I've got proof of my lovability – right here, with them.

We let ourselves in and turn the heating up to thirty to warm up. We put on crazy music and dance around the house, having our own party. One that's not traditionally cool, but cool because we feel free to be truly ourselves. The moon rises higher in the sky, in all its bloody way. It gets to silly o'clock, but we're not sleepy.

"I want to cast one last spell," I declare at two in the morning, "seeing as we're so good at it."

We light candles in my room and I make up the "ingredients" for the spell in my head. I rummage around in the kitchen to find things that represent each of us. Some sugar cubes for Alexis, red grapes for Mia and a vanilla yogurt for me. We put the food in the middle of the circle.

When the magic circle is set, I close my eyes and summon the power that I know is in me. I chant the words to this blessing spell like I've known them my whole life. "Spirits of Mother Nature," I say. "I call on you. I ask that you bless us all and bless our friendship that makes us stronger. Grant us strength in our together and strength in our apart."

"Strength in our together and strength in our apart," my friends repeat.

I share the food between us and we mix the sugar into the yogurt and plop the grapes in. Then we take it in turns to eat it.

"This is so weird," Mia comments, a tablespoon in her mouth. "But, also, all these ingredients totally work together. You've made a new recipe."

"See, I told you. *Ingredients!*" I say.

The Super Blood Wolf Moon looks down on us through my bedroom window as we dissolve into laughter.

TWO AND A HALF YEARS LATER

I stare at the eyeliner pencil, willing it to do what I want it to do.

"Eyeliner, oh eyeliner," I say to the pencil. "Will applying you be overkill with the rest of my outfit?"

Mia emerges from my bathroom, red-faced, wrapped in a towel, big clouds of steam around her. "Talking to inanimate objects again?" she asks.

"At least I've stopped trying to conjure my powers of telekinesis."

Mia laughs as she perches on the edge of

my bed to rough-dry her hair. It will never stop being wonderful that Mia shows off her skin now. She still has scars but no fresh cuts. She's not had those for two and a half years.

"Ha, do you remember our witch phase?" Mia asks, reading my mind. "That was such a fun night."

I watch myself smile at my reflection. "I still can't believe we summoned Alexis's dead dog."

"Oh my God, she HATED that dog. What was that about? Thanks again for letting me use your shower, by the way. I can't believe our boiler broke on the actual night of prom."

"No worries, my dear."

I return to the mirror, trying to figure out if the eyeliner will be too much. I'm still a bit nervous about the dress I've picked. It's so ... not me. Well, so not what people think is me. It's bright red and clingy and you couldn't ignore me in it even if you tried. I've painted my lips ruby red to match.

Mia turns on my hairdryer and blows her hair into submission while I decide a bit of eyeliner isn't going to hurt anyone.

"When's Alexis arriving?" Mia calls over the noise, running her hands through her hair to fluff it. "She's going to make us late, isn't she?"

"Most certainly."

"Pity she's so great."

"I know. A tragedy."

Our witching sleepover all that time ago has been on my mind today. Mainly because I was remembering how certain I'd been that I'd share this moment with Aidan Chambers. What a hilarious thought going to the prom with him is now. It's strange how time can allow you to go from obsessed with someone to completely unbothered by them.

I like time, I decide as I finish a perfect cat-flick with the eyeliner. I like how what's important to you becomes obvious as time passes, because it's the things that stay the same. For example, it's been over two years since that sleepover, and Aidan is just a cringey memory, while my closest friends are still my closest friends.

After she's dried herself off, Mia wiggles into a long black dress that is way too hot and Gothy for summer. But she looks amazing and she's used to wearing black in the heat.

"Are my arms OK?" Mia asks, quickly holding them out. "My scars not too obvious?"

I reflect again on time passing and the good things it can do. Like Mia now being able to have an open and honest conversation about her scars, and not just with us. After that sleepover, Mia even told her parents and they got her to the GP straight away.

"They're fine and you look amazing," I
tell her.

"Cheers, bubs. As do you. Year Nine Sophia
would've never worn red."

"Year Nine Sophia learned to care less what
people think," I reply, smiling.

We turn up the music and shove each other,
fighting for mirror space. Our phones ping at
the same time with a message from Alexis:

TOTAL HAIR DISASTER WILL BE A WHILE

"Always with the drama," Mia says.

"*So* much drama."

"Pity she's so great."

Twenty minutes later, our make-upping is
interrupted by a knock at my door. "Can I come

in yet?" Mum calls. "I need to embarrass you by taking ten million photos."

Typically, Mum doesn't wait for my reply before bounding in. "Oh, Sophia," she says, her hand flying to her mouth. "You look so beautiful."

I blush as red as my dress. "Please don't start crying," I say.

Mum holds up her camera and starts snapping like a crazed paparazzi.

"Mum! I'm not even ready."

"I just want some action shots! OK. Let's go outside and pose."

Mia and I share an eye-roll. "Alexis isn't even here yet," I say.

"We'll get more of the three of you when she arrives," Mum replies. "Come on. Outside. By the tree. Your dad will kill me if I don't get some photos."

I roll my eyes again. "Maybe he should be here if he doesn't want to miss out."

Mum doesn't disagree; instead her lips go thin. That's the sad thing about time passing, I guess. It shows you what's important to you, but, on the flip side, it also shows up how important you are to other people. And my dad has only had me over to visit once since he left for Canada. *Once*.

But I won't let Dad ruin my buzz tonight. I shove my toes into my sandals and hobble downstairs. I catch a glimpse of myself in the hallway mirror and hardly believe it's me.

We head outside and stage a mini photo shoot in the honking sunshine. Mia takes several pictures of Mum and me together. Mum's eyes are misty with pride, like it's my graduation day or something. She keeps saying how proud she is.

"Of what?" I ask.

"Of you being you."

And I find myself hugging her.

Once we're done, Mum yells, "Right, champagne! I'm going to be a terrible influence and let you have a glass before you go." She runs back into the kitchen, powered by her nervous energy.

"You're a legend," Mia calls after Mum, then sits down on one of our garden chairs to rub her already-pinching shoes. "Your mum really is a legend."

I sit down next to Mia. "I know."

We sit in silence for a bit, enjoying the feeling of the early-afternoon sun on our skin. I still can't quite believe school is over. I'll never be in that building ever again. Mia, Alexis and I are all going to the sixth-form college rather than staying on at school, and it can't start quick enough. There will be no more people treating me like I'm the same person I was in Year Seven. A completely fresh start with my oldest and best friends.

"We really did think we were witches, didn't we?" I muse, staring at the bottom of the tree where I'd buried Aidan Chambers and remembering that night.

"We totally were," Mia says. "All of our spells worked. We even resurrected a dog!"

I wag my finger. "Not all of them," I correct her. "My love spell didn't work, remember? Aidan Chambers got back together with stupid non-vegan Jessica Hadley that night when I didn't show at the party." I blow up my fringe and remember weirdly feeling nothing when the photo of Jessica and Aidan kissing appeared on the hashtag. "God, he was a wanker," I add.

"Hmm."

"But if it wasn't for that spell not working, I'd totally have thought we had powers."

"Hmm."

"What's with all the hmming?" I ask, and drag my attention away from a fuzzy bee to turn to Mia. She's randomly gone all red. The blushing stands out against her white skin and she won't look at me.

"What?" I ask. "What is it?"

Mia holds up her hands. "OK, so you have to promise you won't get mad. God! I totally forgot I'd done that!"

"Done *what*? What the hell? Mia? What is it?"

"Promise you won't get mad."

"About something that happened over two years ago?"

"Promise?" Mia demands.

"Yes, jeez! What did you do?"

She doesn't reply straight away but starts scanning around the garden, using her hands to shield her eyes from the sun.

"What?" I ask. "What is it?"

Mum's voice rolls out from the kitchen. "Just putting it on some ice in the sink – five minutes till champagne o'clock."

Mia stands suddenly and hoists her dress up to walk over to the garden shed. She comes back holding a mucky trowel and then squats by the tree and starts digging.

I stand up. "What the hell are you doing? You're going to ruin your dress."

"The thing is," Mia says, ignoring me as she dislodges a lump of soil. I stand up to join her and scoot to one side to avoid getting muddy. "You must understand that my intentions were right. You were so sad after your dad left, and even sadder after Aidan, and I just wanted you to realise how great you are."

I shake my head as Mia lifts up another wormy clod of soil.

"Why the hell are you digging up the garden?" I say.

"Do you not remember the love spell?" Mia asks. "How you had to bury a photo of him?"

"I don't know. I guess ... why ... what ...?"

But I don't finish because Mia's holding up a filthy bit of silk. She flicks it to one side, takes out a very mouldy photo and holds it up. I gasp.

The photo is of me.

Me.

It's my half of the photo I took of me and Aidan. My face.

Not Aidan's face.

"I swapped it when your eyes were closed," Mia says, shrugging and putting the trowel down. "I thought it was more important that you learn to love yourself. To cast a spell that made you realise what *you* are worth rather than giving all your power to a stupid boy."

I reach out and take the photo, stunned. There. There I am. Young Year Nine Sophia, looking fragile and unsure of myself, like I didn't deserve to be holding my cheek next to the boy who was supposed to be buried under this tree.

"I don't know if I should be mad or not," I say.

"I am sorry," Mia replies. "I sort of forgot I'd swapped the photo halves until now."

My mouth drops open. "Hang on, does this mean *all* our spells did work after all? I mean, I did learn to love myself that night. And the dog. And you got help and stopped hurting yourself."

Mia raises both eyebrows. "Maybe. Who knows?"

I feel a chill even though it's boiling hot. I thought that evening was a joke, just young girls being silly. But what if we were—

"Guess who's here?" Mum calls as she arrives on the patio with a tray of full champagne glasses. Alexis stands next to her, looking like she's plugged herself into an electric socket. It distracts me from my train of thought.

"Your hair!" I say to Alexis.

"I KNOW! NOBODY BELIEVED IT WAS BAD BECAUSE YOU ALL THINK I'M DRAMATIC, BUT SOMETIMES I AM ACTUALLY ACCURATE, NOT DRAMATIC."

Mum puts the tray down on the table. "We need photos of this," she says, laughing. "Come on, let me document this disaster, then you can use my fancy straighteners to mend it."

Alexis's hand goes to her crazy head of hair. "I'm not sure I want to document this."

"I promise you these moments are the ones that you really want to remember," Mum says. "Now come on. All together. Group shot!"

We all gather under the same birch tree we stood below two years ago. Grown. Wiser.

Maybe witches, maybe not. I'm not sure if I'll cast a spell again. With friends like this by my side, I'm not sure I'll ever feel the need to.

"Say cheese," Mum tells us.

"Cheeeeeeeese."

The camera clicks and freezes us in time. I think of the girl in that photo, buried under the tree, and how much she'd hated herself. I think of how life got so much better when she started to let go of that hatred and let the love come in. And how it was her friends who helped her get there. The friends whose hands are on my back now, pulling me into them, smiling for my manic mum. And I realise I don't care if we are witches or not. I don't need to know whether or not we are capable of magic. Because learning to love yourself, and finding people who love yourself too, that's the real magic.

Our books are tested
for children and young people by
children and young people.

Thanks to everyone who consulted on
a manuscript for their time and effort in
helping us to make our books better
for our readers.